Obomsawin

of Sioux Junction

Daniel Poliquin

translated by Wayne Grady

Obomsawin

of Sioux Junction

Douglas & McIntyre
Vancouver/Toronto

91 92 93 94 95   5 4 3 2 1

Douglas & McIntyre
1615 Venables Street
Vancouver, British Columbia
V5L 2H1

Canadian Cataloguing in Publication Data
Poliquin, Daniel.
[Obomsawin. English]
Obomsawin of Sioux Junction
Translation of: L'Obomsawin.
ISBN 0-88894-712-7
I. Title. II. Title: Obomsawin. English.
PS8581.O450213 1991   C843'.54   C91-091158-4
PQ3919.2.P5770213   1991

All the characters and events in *Obomsawin of Sioux Junction* are entirely fictional. Any resemblance they may bear to real persons and experiences is illusory.

Originally published in French by Éditions Prise de Parole.

The publisher gratefully acknowledges the assistance of the Canada Council in the publication of this translation.

Cover illustration by Richard da Mota
Cover design by Michael Solomon
Text design by Robert MacDonald/MediaClones
Printed and bound in Canada

1

Obomsawin is dozing off.

By himself, the sole occupant of the only public bench in Sioux Junction, his hometown. Where he's standing trial for arson.

"Public bench" is a manner of speaking: it's really an old pew he dragged there himself after liberating it from the Ukrainian Catholic Church, which closed down long ago, and now he spends nearly all his time on it, waiting for his verdict. "Hometown" is another euphemism, since there isn't much left of Sioux Junction now that the companies have pulled out.

Thomas Obomsawin, painter. There are places where his name still means something. His work is known in every major capital in the world. Two biographies have already been written about him: one by a professor from Toronto, the other by a Montreal art critic.

But Obomsawin hasn't been himself, lately. It's time to rewrite the story of his life. I am his third biographer.

Obomsawin returned to Sioux Junction about a year ago. His life, in fact, has been a litany of forced departures and tolerated returns to the Junction, where he was born and where he'll probably die. He turned up again last year after deciding never to paint again. So far, he's kept his word.

But I think it's fair to say that things haven't gone so well. Thomas Christophe Obomsawin, born December 18, 1935, in Sioux Junction, in the province of Ontario, was charged with arson on April 4, 1985, and bound over to the Supreme Court of Ontario on May 19 following, where he appeared before His Honour Judge James H. Kendrick. Under the Criminal Code, anyone found guilty of voluntarily and deliberately setting fire to a property is liable to fourteen years in prison. Though he seemed to be totally indifferent to the outcome, Obomsawin finally pleaded not guilty. This was largely at the insistence of his lawyer, who managed, not without some difficulty, to convince him of the seriousness of the charges against him. If things go wrong at the trial, he could be looking at a lengthy stretch in the Kingston Pen, or even in the mental hospital in Toronto. Obomsawin keeps telling his lawyer that it doesn't matter, that his life is over anyway, that the lawyer can do what he likes .... Nevertheless, Obom seems to be enjoying the breather that the trial is giving him. He's had time to think about things he'd stopped thinking about years ago. He seems almost happy, as though he were holding three trump cards in his hand—Prison, Hospital and Death. He spends his days shuffling the cards without ever laying them down. He likes the indecision, the haziness. Choices are for later. Maybe the jury will even make the choice for him. We'll soon see.

Sioux Junction's only public bench looks onto Main Street, about half a block down from the Logdrivers Hotel, where the trial is being held. Behind the bench flows the Wicked Sarah River, in which thirteen children have drowned since the founding of the village at the turn of the century. The last drowning—a boy named L'Heureux, who'd been panning for gold in the river because he'd heard that prospectors had once provided the village with a certain measure of prosperity—took place back when the village was under threat of closure: the boy had learned the night before that the mine was being shut down and there was no more work in the woods. He'd got it into his head that if he found gold in the Wicked Sarah, then the prospectors would come back, and with them the mine owners, who were Americans, and the workers and their families, and the penny-goods man who had left a month earlier. At school, he'd learned that the founders of the village had made a fortune when they'd found huge gold nuggets lying in the gravel at the bottom of the Wicked Sarah.

There've been no more children drowned in the river since then. Probably because there've been no more children in Sioux Junction since then.

Two or three times a day Obom makes his way to the bench and waits for his verdict. Some say there never will be a verdict; the trial has been going on for nearly a month. The judge has heard sixty-four witnesses, the Crown and defence attorneys examined and cross-examined Obomsawin himself for more than four full days, and the court has been adjourned three separate times in order to examine certain pieces of evidence *in camera*. And still they aren't finished. There are only thirty people left in Sioux Junction. Twelve of them are on the jury; that doesn't leave a whole lot of people to talk to. You can't talk to the jurors, who naturally are under instructions not to discuss the case. So in order to learn anything new about Obomsawin, you have to go to the eighteen others who are left.

And that isn't as easy as it sounds. Some of them are behind Obom come hell or high water, and swear he's innocent without having very convincing arguments to back them up. Others say he's been a criminal from the day he was born. When you ask one of Obom's supporters what he thinks about the whole thing, he'll tell you: "Obomsawin and his drawings are the pride of Sioux Junction." On the other hand, "Tom Obomsawin makes me sick to my stomach," declares one of his detractors, a man named Roland Provençal. "I've known the bastard since he was this high, and I tell you hanging's too good for him. He's a son of a bitch!" There's no way of knowing who's right.

So Tom came back a year ago and moved into the house that used to belong to his mother, but which the bank had repossessed for back payments. But since there no longer was a bank in Sioux Junction by then, no one said anything about it. He showed up one morning, just like that, without fanfare and without so much as a by-your-leave from anyone. He forced the lock on the door. The house had been empty ever since his mother died six years before. Four days later he had the plumbing working and enough firewood to last him the winter. After that, the village gradually became used to his presence. He hardly went out, except to go for a walk in the village for an hour or so, or to buy a few things at the general store run by Jo Constant at the Logdrivers Hotel. Sometimes he stopped to talk to a friend of his who lived at the hotel.

When I say "hotel" I suppose I'd better be careful again and say right off that in Sioux Junction, some words don't mean the same thing that they mean anywhere else. The Logdrivers has only three rooms, and all the patrons share a common bathroom. It's owned by Jo Constant. Before, when the village was going strong—that is, before the Sauvé brothers' sawmill closed down and the High River Mining Company pulled out—the Logdrivers Hotel had been a pretty prosperous place: the bar had been full from morning till night, and the dining room had been busy too. Now it's even lost its liquor licence. Before the trial, it had only rented out one room all year—to a social worker on a leave of absence for depression, who

9

spends all his time writing. He looks like a walking cadaver. He goes around with a long face and doesn't have a good word to say to anyone except Obomsawin.

Sometimes Obomsawin allowed people to visit his house. That ended, of course, when he set fire to it.

Ever since the fire, Obomsawin has been living in a room Jo Constant and his tub-of-lard of a wife, Cécile, fixed up for him at the Logdrivers. I guess I'd better backtrack a bit. When Obom set fire to his house, it was Jo Constant who arrested him. With so few people left in Sioux Junction, Jo does what is ordinarily done by the authorities: he's the mayor, the sheriff, the bailiff, the justice of the peace and the fire chief all rolled into one, as well as the owner of the only hotel and grocery store in town. Obviously he was never elected to any of those positions, nor has he ever received a cent by way of salary. No one had ever taken him seriously before, but when the village all but closed down for good, he had taken it upon himself to fill the posts simply because somebody had to do it. And he carried out his duties with great pride. It was the first time in his life he had ever felt important.

So when Obomsawin set fire to his house, Jo Constant arrested him. There's never been a proper prison in Sioux Junction, so Constant had designated one of the rooms of his hotel a cell, saying: "I declare this room to be the official prison of Sioux Junction, so get in there, Tom, and remember that from now on you're my prisoner and you can't leave this room without my permission, okay?" Obomsawin, who was drunk as a skunk, cursed him out something fierce, but Jo Constant said to himself: "If he's my prisoner, I can charge the government for his keep; the government will pay me and I can make a little money out of it, which is okay because business hasn't been going too good lately."

The next day, therefore, in his capacity as justice of the peace, Constant had to order Thomas Christophe Obomsawin to stand trial. But he'd have to wake him up first, since the accused was sawing logs in his cell like an old buzz saw. Then, good hotel keeper that he was, he'd have to ask him what he wanted for breakfast. Under the circumstances, so as not to confuse his public duties with his private responsibilities, he asked his wife to go upstairs and find out whether their guest liked his eggs scrambled or sunny-side. His wife, the enormous Cécile, whose tongue was the only sharp thing about her, was having none of that: "You little piece of chicken shit, you're the one who always said it was your job to serve the guests. Now you think you're a big shot, eh? Now you're the la-de-da judge and you think you're too good to do it, eh? Well, read my lips, turkey-face: No way! Go wake up your prisoner yourself. I've got my own work to do. I've got food to prepare, that's my job. You go do your job. For once we've got a paying customer in this place who might stay longer than it takes to drink a cup of coffee, and you start acting like a judge instead of a hotel keeper! Get going!" And in order to keep the peace, Jo got going. "Okay," he said, "but you're going to do the washing up. I can't do everything around here, dammit!"

After reading Thomas Christophe Obomsawin the charges against him as set down by Sheriff Constant and Chief of Police Constant, Justice of the Peace Constant ordered the accused to appear before the court. He did this as soon as Hotel Keeper Constant had awakened his guest, whose only response was to turn back over in bed and, in a voice unmistakably that of someone who had had too much to drink the night before, say: "Not so loud, Jo, I've got a headache. I'll come down later. I'm tired." To which Jo replied: "No problem, Tom. Court opens at nine o'clock, but you can show up whenever you like. I've got no one else to see but you today, anyway."

This didn't exactly sit well with Jo's wife, who recognized a shirker when she saw one. She told her husband to run Obomsawin out of town, like they used to do in the good old days before the

Junction had a prison. As a citizen, she had the right to insist that the police rid her town of rubbies who set fire to their own houses for no good reason; and as chief magistrate, it was Jo's duty to carry out the wishes of the populace. Constant gravely invited his wife to drop by his office sometime, where he would consider her request with all due respect. That didn't sit well with her, either. She told Jo to get lost: "You think because you peel potatoes in the same sink as me you can play the big magistrate too, eh? Okay, so don't listen to me; at least you don't have to piss me off. Just throw the idiot out, why can't you? I suppose that's asking too much too, eh, you wimp?"

Though somewhat unnerved by this at first, Constant managed to reply that, wimp or no wimp, the case was now in the hands of the court, and that no matter what anyone thought about Obomsawin, he was entitled to a fair and equitable trial. It fell to him, as justice of the peace, to maintain Public Order, but also to see that the accused was treated fairly. It was his bounden duty: he, Joseph Constant, was the Representative of Justice in Sioux Junction, and it wouldn't do to allow his Obligations as a Landlord to interfere with his Responsibilities as a Public Servant. It would be held against him.

"You do what you like," said his wife, "but I'm not serving him no breakfast in bed, you can take that to the bank. The lazy good-for-nothing!"

Sensing that she was calming down, Constant promised her he would do what he had to do as the hotel's proprietor. He also promised he would call the Crown attorney's office in Thunder Bay to arrange for the trial and receive further instructions. After all, she had to admit, this was the first time in his career that anything this big had ever landed in his lap.

Madame Constant was mollified: "That's true enough, God knows. Go and ask him what he wants for breakfast."

After serving Obom his summons as the sheriff of Sioux

Junction, Constant asked him whether he wanted pancakes or bacon and eggs for breakfast.

Obom: "Just toast and coffee, Jo."

Jo: "Very good, Obom, I'll bring them up for you right away. Meanwhile, if you want a shower it's at the end of the hallway. If you need anything else, just holler. But come down to the dining room when you're finished. That's where I have my court set up."

Around eleven o'clock, after a good night's sleep and a light breakfast, Obomsawin made his way down to the dining room on the ground floor, where he found Jo Constant, wearing his regulation black gown, waiting to read him his charges. After he had read them, he asked: "Thomas Christophe Obomsawin, do you plead guilty or not guilty to the charges as set before you?" To which Obom replied: "There's no soap in the shower, Jo, and I'll have another order of toast and coffee. And some more of that gooseberry jam your wife made. It tastes pretty good."

Jo Constant pondered this for a minute. Should he take the opportunity to make a bit more money from the government, or should he uphold the Dignity of the Law of Canada in Sioux Junction? He gave it another moment's thought, then rapped twice on the dining-room table with his gavel: "The accused may finish his breakfast while the court adjourns to read up on what procedure it has to follow in cases like this." So saying, he rose with great dignity and exited through the door to the kitchen. (He had spoken his final words in English, because English has always been the Language of Justice in Ontario, but when he'd taken off his black robe and put on his apron, he suddenly remembered that criminal courts are now officially allowed to hear cases in French, if the accused so desires; he'd read about it in the Thunder Bay newspaper only the other day.) So then, changing his mind, he whipped off his apron, put his robe back on, and went back into the dining room–cum–courtroom where Obomsawin was yawning so hard it looked like he was trying to swallow a horse. Resuming his place at the head table, in front of his minutes and the gavel, Jo gave the table a rap and said, in English: "Does the accused want a trial in French?" To which Obomsawin replied: "Yes, as soon as you bring me two eggs and bacon. It's getting late and I'm hungry."

Judge Constant made a note in his minutes: " 'The accused requested a trial in French and two eggs with bacon.' Scrambled or sunny-side, Tom? The eggs, I mean."

"Sunny-side."

"Okay, now, do you want a trial by judge only, or by judge and jury? It doesn't make any difference to me. A jury'll take longer, though. You think about it while I go get your eggs. Sunny-side, you said?"

When Jo called the Crown attorney's office in Thunder Bay, he had a hard time making himself understood. No one there had ever heard of him, and the receptionist didn't even know where Sioux Junction was. She didn't have time to talk with him anyway; there were four trials on the rolls that morning already. He'd have to call her back tomorrow.

Constant was ticked off. Not that he took himself so seriously, but justice was justice, after all, and he had an accused criminal on his hands who looked like he was going to plead not guilty. This was serious business, and they couldn't even find Sioux Junction on the map. Sioux Junction had been an important town in its day. He had half a mind to say the hell with it and send Obomsawin home with a reprimand. But his wife, who had had time to think the whole thing over, wouldn't hear of that: why throw out a good customer whose tab was being picked up by the government? And if the case was heard here in Sioux Junction, it would probably bring in even more customers. If ever there was a golden opportunity, this was it, and God knows opportunities don't grow on trees. And so on and so on, the same song she'd been singing for seven years. To get some peace, Jo told her he'd call the Crown attorney's office back in the morning.

But she was on a roll. Following him into his office, she continued to light into him, harping on the same theme she dredged up every time she had a chance. She called it pouring her heart out.

Jo had retired from Falconbridge Mines in Sudbury seven years earlier, after thirty years of good and faithful service. His children were all grown up and married off. So he sold his house, withdrew his life savings from the Caisse Populaire and bought the Logdrivers Hotel in Sioux Junction for a song. He wanted to keep busy in his retirement, and he had always dreamed of owning his own hotel and restaurant. Having worked for other people all his life, he wanted to work for himself for a change. An old dream of being a success in life: having his own business, working when he felt like it, sleeping in anytime he wanted to, being his own boss, giving orders, letting other people work for him, spending the whole winter in Florida. The good life!

Three months after he retired, he'd gone on a fishing trip to Manitoba. After passing through Thunder Bay, he'd got lost and found himself in Sioux Junction, a village he'd only vaguely heard of before. He liked the area, and ended up staying at the Logdrivers Hotel for two days. In the bar that first night, the hotel's owner, a Syrian, had told him about his plans to sell the hotel and move back to Vancouver to join his cousins. He gave poor Jo his dinner on the house, which made Jo feel rich and important: at last, he thought, here was the kind of business he'd always dreamed of owning. On that particular night the bar had been full of drinkers and business had seemed to be booming. Constant thought the situation over and clinched the deal on the spot, without even calling his wife, who, he knew, would be as delighted as he was.

When he got home, his wife came down on him like a ton of

bricks. She didn't want to hear about any hotel, he should have talked to her about it first. "All my life," he said to himself, "people have thought of me as a wimp, that I could never manage my own business. Well, no more! I'm gonna show them what I'm made of." And he held his ground. He broke down his wife's resistance with three basic arguments: first, at this price—fifteen thousand dollars for the building and all its equipment—the place was a steal; second, the numbers looked good, the customers were quiet and paid cash; and finally, there was no competition. They could charge what they liked. They could even close up for the winter and go to Florida! In the end, his wife had said yes. But she had her doubts.

And she was right. Jo and Cécile Constant took possession of the Logdrivers Hotel and, upright, serious folk that they were, launched into a frenzy of spring cleaning. They didn't have much choice, since the Syrian had been a real pig, according to Cécile. Still, all the kitchen and baking equipment was in working order. Jo decided to wait until the following year to expand, a decision his wife loudly decried: "If you think you're going to make a living out of three rooms, you're crazy in the head, you poor little bugger." Jo had long been used to hearing his wife talk to him like that, though, and didn't bother listening to her. This time, maybe he should have.

When everything was ready, the Constants planned their official grand opening under new management. Cécile put cut flowers on all the tables in the dining room, and invited the children and their families down from Sudbury. None of the children could make it, unfortunately; previous commitments, they said. Cécile grumbled loudly about that: they could have made an effort, after all. Sioux Junction wasn't the end of the world, you know! The worst betrayal was yet to come, however: no one from Sioux Junction came to the opening either, despite the printed notices Jo had distributed around the village. No one. Not a soul. On the night of the hotel's grand opening, Jo and Cécile ate alone, talking together at a small table in the big dining room, something they hadn't done since they were first married. "Don't go getting any grand ideas about this place," Cécile told her husband. She was on a slow boil. "Here we are with a kitchen full of food on our hands and not a soul in the bar. We won't make a cent out of this place tonight!"

Cécile was still raging the next day. Jo had gone around asking a few questions. What the Syrian had forgotten to tell them was that the village was in the process of being closed down. The sawmill was down to five employees and the High River iron-ore mine wasn't far behind. The price of iron ore had plummeted on the Toronto Stock Exchange, and lumber sales were soft because high interest rates had put the skids under new house construction. Which was why the Sauvé brothers, who had been taking a beating on the sawmill for years already, had finally decided to shut down the plant and give their land back to the Crown.

It didn't take Jo Constant long to figure it out: "I've been fucked in the ear by a goddamned Syrian bastard!" To the people who remained in the village, he said: "Why didn't you tell me this when I was going around with my posters, inviting you all to the grand opening with open arms?" There was a general shuffling of feet at this; they were too embarrassed to reply. Finally, Roland Provençal explained it to him: "You poor bugger, we figured you'd take it too much to heart. We thought maybe you still had hopes that the village would go back to the way it was. We didn't want to make you feel bad."

Jo almost cried at that. "Well anyway," he said, "you could have come to the opening, you didn't have to leave us all alone like that, me with the wife."

"You don't understand, Jo," they said. "What d'you think we were gonna use for money? We can't afford to drink at your hotel. We don't have money for drinking and dancing, like we had before. No one here has a red cent. That's why we didn't come." Jo went sadly back to the hotel, where his wife was still going on. He spent the night alone in the bar, drinking the rye and beer he had got in to sell to his customers.

Fat Cécile rumbled like a volcano for a time, but gradually she subsided. Jo kept pretty much to himself. They stayed on. Together, through the windows of their empty hotel, they waved good-bye to the rest of Sioux Junction as, one by one, the townspeople all left to find work somewhere else.

Right from the start, Cécile had been embarrassed at having Obomsawin stay at the Logdrivers: it was the first time the hotel had had anyone in it since the grand opening. And even at that he couldn't be an ordinary guest, like the tourists who used to come to Sioux Junction for the trout fishing or the bear hunting. Not him. He was staying there against his will, with the government paying his bill as long as he was a prisoner on trial. Which meant, in reality, that the Logdrivers wasn't even a hotel any more. It was a prison! Her complaints became longer and heavier than usual. Her husband ignored them.

Jo never complained. Why should he, as his wife never failed to point out: the whole thing was his fault. He should have asked her first, but since he hadn't bothered, she'd better not hear him griping about it now! But Jo didn't see it that way at all. For him, the Logdrivers Hotel was a cheap retirement home as well as a sort of pastime. He had plenty of time to go fishing and hunting, winter or summer, no clients to bother him and so much the better for that! His only problem was his wife, who complained about being so far out in the bush that the children never came to see them. She would've liked it better in a real hotel, she said, one that held conferences and had interesting guests and a bar full of miners and lumberjacks who drank like fish. Maybe not for a long time, but long enough to see what it was like. Instead, what did she have? A hotel that didn't even have a licence—they had forgotten to renew it two years ago. And a building that wasn't worth a plug nickel any more.

Sioux Junction started shutting down shortly after their arrival here, and their official reopening became something of a local joke. Nearly every day for two years they watched families pack up their things and drive off, kids howling and laughing at the same time.

The miners left first. High River Mines had decided to sink an ore shaft somewhere else, in Asia maybe, where people didn't mind hard work and never went on strike. Most of the mine workers found other jobs without much trouble, at Elliot Lake or in Timmins. The workers at the Sauvé brothers' sawmill followed suit about a year later.

The men left first, and their families joined them after a few months when the kids were out of school, or something like that. For a while, it looked as though Sioux Junction were a town inhabited entirely by women and children. Then even they left, following their fathers' footsteps. One by one, the company houses built along the banks of the Wicked Sarah became empty. Nobody bought them.

The whole world had given up on Sioux Junction, it seemed. Even the parish priest, who had said he wouldn't budge as long as there was one Catholic soul left in Sioux Junction. One morning he folded up his tent like all the rest. Poor man, he had tears in his eyes: he had no choice, he said. Every Sunday there were fewer and fewer people at mass; no more funerals, no more baptisms, the collection was too small to pay for the upkeep of the church. The year before he left, he had organized a lottery, the profits from which he'd promised to use to advertise the village to potential investors from outside. This, said the priest, would revitalize the economy. The grand prize was a brand-spanking-new Cadillac, and the winning ticket had been purchased by the nun who cooked in the presbytery. She had given the Cadillac to the priest, who promised to resell it and donate the money to the Sioux Junction Catholic Mission. Unfortunately, he couldn't find anyone in Sioux Junction who could afford to buy a Cadillac, even though in the old days there'd been miners who'd bought Caddies with their overtime pay. Now nobody wanted it. The priest left on a Sunday morning, right after mass. During his sermon, he had told the last of his flock that he had done everything he could, but that God had willed it otherwise. Afterwards, as he drove off in his Cadillac, he had waved good-bye to his tearful parishioners.

Another thing the priest had said in his final sermon was that he was being replaced by another priest, a young curate fresh out of Thunder Bay, who would do for this parish everything that the old priest could have done and more. He wasn't coming right away, though, but later on, when the diocese could afford it. The diocese could never afford it, so it seemed, for the young curate never did show up.

Then the school principal left. And the butcher. And the baker. And the guy who owned the general store. Everyone left. Constant, with his hotel and his fat wife who never stopped complaining about always getting the dirty end of the stick, was the only businessman left in the village. He started a little grocery store in the back of his hotel because, as he said, people had to eat. He opened up once a week and, thank God, he didn't overcharge. For there were still people in Sioux Junction: people on social assistance, senior citizens who had nowhere else to go, and others like Roland Provençal, who said he'd done enough moving in his life and that Sioux Junction was his last stop. And there were a few Indians who came into town from time to time, stayed for a few months and then left, old-timers who used to come down more often when the town was more prosperous.

The Indians were never up to much. Never up to much good, anyway, if you listened to Roland Provençal. They'd go on binges— drinking contraband liquor — after moving into one or another of the abandoned company houses along the river. Then they'd leave and come back again. Sometimes they'd fight among themselves, but no one ever arrested them because there was no longer a uniformed cop in town.

When the town was all but empty the senior citizens asked Jo Constant to take on some of the public positions so that a semblance of law and order could be maintained. Jo accepted willingly. He'd never held any sort of office before. Cécile called him His Wartship or the Sergeant Mayor when she was mad at him, just to get him going. But he didn't laugh. He took his duties seriously.

So, there aren't a lot of people left in Sioux Junction. Two years ago, a social worker from the University of Toronto wandered into the area with the idea of studying the lifestyle of the local native peoples, or something to that effect. After a year he had a nervous breakdown and moved into the Logdrivers Hotel. From then on, everyone called him the Great Depression.

And then Obomsawin came back. The crazy son of a bitch who set fire to his own house and nobody knew why.

2

Some of Obomsawin's earliest paintings depict the history of Sioux Junction.

The town can scarcely be said to exist any more. Look at any of the tourist maps published by the province of Ontario, and you won't find Sioux Junction on them anywhere. You'd have to consult one of the topographical maps put out by the federal department of Energy, Mines and Resources to see that it still has a name. Otherwise, nothing. The place has been discarded like an old apple core.

When Obomsawin let his talent as an artist be known, his first big commissions came from the township council, which in those days could still afford to support an official painter and wanted, in its wisdom, to immortalize the history of the town in oil. Obomsawin was about twenty-five years old then, more or less half his present age.

Obomsawin's first biographer wrote that his debut as an artist was as a historical painter. This isn't true. Obom painted those tableaux merely in order to eat, not for any artistic reasons. He had just returned from a long trip to Germany, and he had been in prison. He was broke and needed to buy food. So he agreed to paint the town's history in order to earn some money.

These paintings, the ones I'm talking about now, were all kept in the house belonging to his mother, which had been taken over by Obomsawin. They were burned in the fire. That's why Obom is a wanted man in Sioux Junction: some of the citizens, Roland Provençal among them, had wanted to turn the house into a museum. Obomsawin was famous from Moscow to Washington. Maybe they could have made some money from him, you never know, maybe even got the town back on its feet. Now there's nothing left of the house or the paintings except ashes and the testimonies of a few eyewitnesses.

Anyway, I should tell you what those early official paintings of Sioux Junction recorded. As his third biographer, I'm one of the few people in the world who has seen them.

The first tableau depicted the founders of Sioux Junction: Charlemagne Ferron and Byron Miles.

The first panel showed them side by side: Byron Miles, wearing the slightly soiled tunic of the North West Mounted Police, kneeling beside the Wicked Sarah panning for gold with a prospector's pan; in the background, Charlemagne Ferron turning over earth with a shovel, the sleeves of his Mackinaw shirt rolled up, his eyes fixed on the fresh soil.

It was the end of the last century. Charlemagne was from Quebec—Saint-Ours-sur-Richelieu, to be exact. In his younger days he had been a priest, something the good citizens of Sioux Junction didn't like to admit later on: that the French founder of their town had been an apostate, a defrocked priest. His biographical note in the town archives is formally worded: "Charlemagne Ferron, ordained in the Diocese of Quebec on May 4, 1897, at the age of 23; completed his studies in the Seminaire de Québec and, once ordained, went out to the St. Pierre of Montana Mission in the United States. There, after ministering to Indians and Metis, including the great Louis Riel, he unfortunately renounced his vocation." He had only taken holy orders to please his father, after all, who'd been a big farmer back east, surrounded by power and priests who always bought up his entire crop of oats. One of Charlemagne's flock denounced him to the Bishop of Chicago after finding him *in flagrante delicto* with a young Blackfoot girl, to whom he had been teaching French and natural science.

Rather than reply to the summons of his bishop, who had ordered him to Chicago, Father Ferron fled. He spent some time working as a printer in St. Louis, Missouri, but ran into difficulties there with the parish priest, who was a French-Canadian and who continually reproached Ferron for, among other things, his weakness for alcohol and saloon girls. Once again he decamped, this time to Texas. He settled in a small Methodist border town, where he married and became an American citizen, a Methodist and a rancher. For several years he drove herds of cattle to feed himself and his family—he had had one or two children; the records are unclear. His wife died of typhoid fever; his children too, probably— here, too, the records are ambiguous. We do know, however, that all his worldly goods were lost in a fire. Ferron left again, this time heading north, leaving behind him all traces of his ecclesiastical past and bringing with him only his knowledge of modern American agricultural practices.

Back in Canada, he worked mostly in the forest as a lumberjack, and purchased—for next to nothing—a vast tract of Crown land in northern Ontario. Included in the transaction was a large section of arable land situated on the banks of the Wicked Sarah.

I should mention at this point that upon his arrival in Canada, Ferron had looked up a former fellow seminarian, who had become a curate and was living in Toronto. This worthy priest had absolved

Ferron of his sins and had instructed him to do penance for his
errant ways by working on the land and founding a family that
would further the cause of French Canada. Ferron promised
nothing, but his friend's instructions fit in with his inclinations, for
he had developed a yen for farming in a region far removed from
civilization. He wanted to start a town. Hence his purchase of the
Crown land. There was, of course, no question of his returning to
Quebec, where his past was well known, and so the land he bought
was in Ontario, north of Lake Superior. It was a place where he
could begin his life anew, and conduct it any way he wanted. In
Toronto, when the clerk at the Ministry of Agriculture had handed
him his deed, he had promised in return to build a homestead, to
clear an acre of land a year for three years and to "favour coloniza-
tion."

He kept his word. Before Charlemagne Ferron, there was
nothing at all on the banks of the Wicked Sarah. Ferron built a log
cabin, by himself, with his bare hands. Then he marked off where
his fields would be, ready for clearing. After a year he began to run
short of supplies, and he returned to Toronto to restock. When he
got back, he found a tall, blond man dressed in a worn red tunic
living in his cabin. The tunic was the uniform of the North West
Mounted Police, and the blond man said he was a licenced constable
turned prospector and that his name was Byron Miles. He spoke in
broken English—Ferron noticed it right away, but reserved his
questions for later. The man had obviously not eaten for days. He
had been panning in the river for several months, and did not know
how to hunt. Ferron offered to share his flour, beans and pork, and
the tall, blond man in the scarlet tunic solemnly promised to repay
him one day, as soon as he struck the mother lode he had been
dreaming of.

Sioux Junction's self-righteous anglophone community never
actually acknowledged the fact that the cofounder of their town had

been a deserter from the North West Mounted Police. Time ennobles pioneers. Nevertheless, Obomsawin's canvases clearly stated the truth: the rosary under Ferron's foot, for example, and the red tunic worn by the prospecting Miles.

Byron Miles—a good English name, and the one he is known by today—was Ukrainian by origin, from Kiev, where he'd been a boot maker named Balthazar Szepticky. Szepticky may have been a common enough name in the old country, but it was a totally unpronounceable mishmash in the offices of the immigration authorities who processed him and the boatload of other Ukrainian peasants who came clamouring to farm the Canadian West. It was the era of frontiersmanship in Alberta and Saskatchewan. Balthazar, who had one or two marks against him in the Ukraine—refusing his military service under the Russian flag, for one—heeded the call of the chief of his native village of Dnieprovok, who appealed to his persecuted brothers to emigrate to Canada. Balthazar left one night through the green border, without telling anyone in his family where he was going for fear of reprisals from the police.

Balthazar Szepticky had learned boot making from his father, and quite obviously knew nothing about agriculture. The entire village of Dnieprovok was intending to farm in the New World but they agreed to take Balthazar along with them anyway. He was a strong young man with an ambitious nature, and they could always use an extra pair of hands. Besides, who knows, when they got the village going on Canadian soil, they might need a boot maker. So Balthazar made the trip on nothing more than his strong arms and his good looks; even at that, he had to pay his way by promising to work for the chief for two years without wages. It was a deal.

Balthazar spent the entire journey acting as a kind of servant to the chief. He carried his luggage, ran all his errands for him. Secretly, he had determined to part company with his fellow peasants as soon as they left the Ukraine, maybe in Germany. But their route took them through Turkey instead, and he had no desire to remain in the same country with a bunch of Turks. He decided to wait for a better opportunity. Maybe America. There was another reason he waited: he had fallen in love with the chief's granddaughter, Natalka, who was thirteen years old. Balthazar spent the entire voyage torn between his desire to flee and his longing to be with the beautiful Natalka.

When the ship docked in Halifax, Balthazar decided to throw in his lot with the new Ukraine they were going to establish in Canada, and he popped the question to the chief, who turned him down flat. If the young man wanted Natalka's hand in marriage, he said, he would first have to fulfil his promise to work the new land for two years, free; that way, he would show his future in-laws that he was a man of his word. If things went well, the chief might give his consent. Balthazar's determination to flee was rekindled; it took all of Natalka's sighs, all her ardent promises that one day she would be his wife, to make him stay. Once he had made his decision, however, he suffered patiently: after all, the two years would pass quickly, he wasn't twenty yet, he had lots of time.

The caravan continued west. During the trip, Balthazar earned the respect of his compatriots. The elders accepted him as a member of the village. He made himself useful to everyone: he picked up English quickly, and as soon as he learned a few new words, he sat down and taught them to the youngsters. He was also one of the few émigrés who could read; it fell to him to straighten things out with the immigration authorities, who began making difficulties as soon as the group arrived in Canada. He learned a useful lesson in Halifax, from a remark made by one of the immigration officers: "Szepticky," the agent had said. "How the hell do you pronounce that name? This is British country, my boy. Do yourself a favour and drop that stupid name of yours. If you're smart, you'll do it and the future will be yours." Balthazar remembered the advice.

The trip west passed without incident. Not much to relate. Montreal, Toronto, Chicago, Minneapolis, and from there the long trek north by prairie schooner. Balthazar remained with the group, and in love with Natalka. The chief was already treating him like a son. The Canadian government had given the former residents of Dnieprovok a concession in Saskatchewan, a place called Buffalo Hill. There was no one there except an agent of the provincial agriculture and immigration ministry, whose job was solely to divvy up the parcels of land among the newcomers. As soon as that was done, he left. The Ukrainians had been given provisions for two years, some farming equipment and a few horses. They set to work without delay.

Balthazar had never worked so hard in his life. But he took to farm work like a duck to water. Before the year was out the first seeds were in the ground; houses had sprung up everywhere. The chief was still the chief, and Natalka was fifteen: Balthazar had only one year left to wait.

Balthazar kept his word to the chief. When two years and one day had passed since the caravan of Ukrainian immigrants had arrived in Buffalo Hill, the chief called Balthazar to him, blessed him, and gave thanks to the Almighty for sending such a dutiful servant and perhaps even a devoted son who would marry his beloved Natalka. Balthazar thanked his master on both knees, and then announced his immediate departure. He no longer wanted to marry Natalka, who at any rate was in love with someone else. "I forgive her, father," said Balthazar. "We weren't really suited to each other anyway, and besides, who would want a penniless man like myself for a husband? Let her marry someone else, someone who will make her happy. To be honest, master, though I feel very strong bonds with the people of Dnieprovok, I feel an even stronger desire to see the world. Now that I've fulfilled my obligations to you, it's time to go. Back home in the Ukraine, the judge condemned me to three months penal servitude in Siberia; here, I have served a much longer sentence—but it has been for you, and you have treated me like your own son. Now I am free. Give me your blessing, father, for I am about to embark on a long voyage."

The chief was shattered, but he gave Balthazar his blessing, along with five dollars and enough provisions for a month. Then the whole village accompanied the young adventurer to the road leading south, and wished him good luck on his journey.

Balthazar didn't journey very far. In fact, he headed straight for Regina, on foot, and enlisted in the North West Mounted Police, also known as the Redcoats.

The recruiting officer was a sergeant major named Carruthers, a big Englishman with a Lancashire accent and ten years' service in the Indian Army under his belt. Tough as nails, a firm believer in the British Empire's divine mission to civilize the world, full moustache on his stiff upper lip, scarlet tunic impeccably starched. Balthazar seemed a worthy candidate for the mounted police: he was big, strong, used to hard work, familiar with the area and he knew how to ride a horse. Carruthers presented him with a contract that offered him three hundred dollars a year, payable every six months, as well as free room and board. In return, the new conscript agreed to conduct himself in a manner befitting a loyal servant of Her Majesty Queen Victoria, Queen of England and the Dominion of Canada, and Empress of India.

Carruthers hesitated only once while he was filling out Balthazar's papers, and that was at the line marked "Name of Recruit." He told the young man in no uncertain terms that his name was barbarous. "Nobody in his right mind would pronounce that horrendous name, let alone write it," he said. "Besides, Her Majesty doesn't need any Russian servants. Remember, once you wear the scarlet uniform you embody the might of the British Crown. Nobody will take you seriously with a name like ... that."

Balthazar thought a moment and recalled the name of the immigration officer who had told him more or less the same thing when he had arrived in Halifax; the officer's name, he remembered, was Byron Miles. So Balthazar signed the contract Byron Miles, a name he would carry for the rest of his life. When Carruthers checked the recruit's signature, he gave a little smile of satisfaction: "Very well, young man."

From then on, Balthazar Szepticky—or Byron Miles to his friends—taught himself to speak English with a proper British accent, not always with the happiest results. His desire to master his new mother tongue was so strong that he automatically adopted the speech patterns of some of his colleagues in the force, not all of whom were British, and all that became mixed in with his own Ukrainian accent, which steadfastly refused to disappear.

He got through his basic training without difficulty. He learned the correct way to mount and care for a horse, how to shoot a rifle, how to apply the laws of the British Empire in Canada and how to abide by the rules of the mounted police. His first year went very well. He became friendly with the Cree and Blackfoot tribes that lived in the region; he arrested a few smugglers hauling American whiskey across the border; and, above all, he learned how to survive on his own out on the lone prairie. His superiors were happy with his progress.

It couldn't last, of course. One day he was ordered to arrest a Blackfoot named White Wolf, a man who had saved his life during a bear hunt just one month before. White Wolf had his faults, it was true—among other things, he had just murdered a Scottish settler who had fallen in with a group of American smugglers. And since murder was a crime, White Wolf had to be brought to justice without delay, and the officer in charge of the Sky Hill Detachment, a certain Corporal Prendergast, had ordered Constable Byron Miles to bring White Wolf in dead or alive. Just the week before, the same

Corporal Prendergast had put Miles on charge for an infraction of the dress code—a grease spot on his uniform—and Miles, having failed to pass his bimonthly inspection, had had his pay for the past three months cut in half. And now this good-for-nothing Prendergast—a native of Warsaw, whose real name was Scherlowski—was ordering him to arrest a friend, almost a brother, whose only crime had been to rid the region of a worthless scum of a rumrunner. Miles accepted the mission, however, and rode off, with the firm intention of never coming back.

When Miles caught up with White Wolf, he told him to get his ass out of the country as swiftly as possible. By way of thanks, White Wolf gave him some prospecting equipment he had stolen from the Scotsman. This gave Miles the idea of going to Alaska to search for gold. When he struck it rich, he would go back to Europe and set himself up in Paris, or even Heidelberg, and hang around with high society pretending to be a wealthy Englishman. And maybe sail around the world.

If Byron Miles thought he had worked hard and suffered much in his life so far, he hadn't seen anything yet. First he had to shake off his colleagues in the mounted police, who wanted to bring him in for dereliction of duty, fraternizing with criminal elements and desertion. He reached the American border after suffering incredible hardships, only to have his prospecting equipment stolen from him in St. Louis: the cowboys who lightened his load figured rightly that a deserter from the Mounties wouldn't be too quick to go to the police.

With no money, no family and no friends, Byron Miles did as thousands of others have done: he started from scratch. He devoted himself to the fur and whiskey trades, taking up with a ring of traffickers to whom he taught the ways of avoiding the mounted police border patrols. After five months he was able to re-equip himself and once again was ready to set off for Alaska. What stopped him from going this time was nineteen years old, had blonde hair, green eyes and a sprinkling of freckles on a background of perfect white. Her name was Rhian; she had been born in Wales and had come to the United States with her family, all the men of which worked as lumberjacks in the huge sawmills of Minnesota. Miles met her during a stopover near Minneapolis, fell in love with her, and immediately begged her to marry him. She accepted, and their engagement was announced a month later. Byron set aside his prospecting gear in order to take up the lumbering trade with Rhian's brothers, who were all jolly good chaps when they weren't drunk, which wasn't often. Byron wanted to become an honest man again and to earn enough money as a lumberjack to take him to Alaska—not as a poor prospector, this time, but as a married man with a family to support.

Once again he changed his plans, but this time it was for the better. One of Rhian's brothers told him that there was more gold in the rivers of northern Ontario than in all the hills of Alaska and the Yukon put together. And life in the far north would be a lot more difficult. Byron also figured that travelling to Ontario would be quicker and therefore less expensive, and he could chuck off his past as a Mountie there just as easily as anywhere else. Later, when he had found his pile of gold, he would send for Rhian—which would be a lot more complicated from Alaska.

Byron packed up his still-new prospecting gear and took to the road. It was not a smooth one. When Charlemagne Ferron found him sleeping in his cabin, Byron was half dead from exhaustion and hunger. After four months of sloshing through the rivers of the frozen north, he hadn't turned up a single speck of gold, and he had begun to wonder whether Rhian's brothers hadn't sent him up here just to get rid of him because he wasn't Welsh.

So his heart was bitter when he made the acquaintance of Charlemagne Ferron, who told him outright that his chances of finding gold anywhere in northern Ontario were practically nil. Ferron advised him to seek his fortune some other way. For starters, he could get rid of his mounted police uniform, which would undoubtedly get him into hot water before very long.

It must be noted that the two men got on famously as soon as they met and shared their innermost secrets with each other. For example, Charlemagne told Byron about his past as a defrocked priest. It was the beginning of a friendship that would never die. Ferron willingly shared his provisions and tools with Miles, who in turn made his host's life infinitely easier by helping him clear fields and chop wood, two occupations he knew well. Only one thing bothered Ferron: having to speak English all the time. Byron promised to learn French, and Ferron asked to be taught some Ukrainian during the long nights of their first winter together. But nothing much came of these efforts. Miles had used up all of his linguistic talents learning English, and taking up a third language now was more than he was capable of. What was more, he had begun to lose his Ukrainian. Ferron didn't push it, and so their common language remained English.

During their first winter together, Ferron taught Miles how to trap and, in return, Miles finished the inside of Ferron's cabin. He also cut all the firewood; this gave him the idea of constructing a sawmill, with which they could supply the rapidly expanding American market for newsprint. Rhian's brothers had talked continuously about such a scheme, and Miles was convinced they could have gone far with the idea if they hadn't spent all their time drinking away their pay at the local saloon. If he, Byron Miles, could succeed in realizing their dreams, he would surely be held in high esteem by his in-laws, and the green-eyed Rhian would be proud of him—maybe even love him more than ever. He mentioned this project to Ferron, who encouraged him wholeheartedly to go ahead with it. He would need someone with some business sense who knew how to go about setting these sorts of things up, Ferron told him, and he would have to go to Toronto to obtain the necessary cutting rights for Crown land, make the administrative arrangements and so on. Miles promised to make Ferron a partner in his new venture.

The following spring an event took place that upset their apple cart just a little. While out hiking in the woods, Miles came upon a young Native woman all but dead from starvation. She was a Sioux who had spent the previous four years as a slave in a Cree camp near Lake Dryden, in the north. When food became scarce in the camp, she was an extra mouth to feed, and the Cree had pushed her out to fend for herself. She had headed south, alone, after being beaten mercilessly in case she should have the nerve to think about returning to the camp. She hadn't had a bite to eat in four days. She could hardly speak, and she seemed very frightened. Miles brought her back to the cabin and fixed her a meal. Ferron joined them later that evening, and heard her story as translated by Miles, who still knew a few words of Sioux from his sojourn out west.

The two men invited the little Sioux to move in with them, and together the three came to an agreement. When she had recovered, she could leave if she wanted to, or she could stay on as their housekeeper. Neither Ferron nor Miles ever managed an English translation of her name, though, so Ferron took to calling her Obomsawin, after an Abenaki girl he had known back in Saint-Ours-sur-Richelieu, of whom he retained several fond memories. The name stuck.

And of course, the inevitable happened. Both men set about seducing little Obomsawin as soon as she was better. The girl refused neither of them; she wasn't used to having her permission asked before being raped. When either Miles or Ferron made advances to her, she just lay back, stared up at the ceiling and waited to be pounced upon. The pouncing usually took place during the day, never at night, because the two men needed their sleep. No one knows who had had the first pounce, the Anglicized Ukrainian North West Mounted Police deserter or the defrocked French-Canadian priest. It remained their secret.

And naturally, the inevitable happened again. Nine months later, a child was born to the three of them—a boy. Obomsawin delivered it herself, in the woods. She had been pregnant twice before, but both times the baby had been stillborn. This time her child lived, and it had two fathers. Obomsawin decided to stay with the men and raise her child. After that, however, nothing was the same among them; it was as if the young woman ceased to exist in the men's eyes. They seemed ill at ease around her, possibly because of the child.

For the rest, life went on. Byron Miles had taken Ferron's advice to heart. He had gone to Toronto and purchased the cutting rights to all the Crown land in the area. Then, again on Ferron's advice, he had borrowed money from the bank, hired workers, bought material and found buyers for his wood. Meanwhile, Charlemagne Ferron got his first crops off the land and into the barn. The little Sioux had more children. She had named the first one Francis Obomsawin; he was the painter's grandfather.

Before long there were a lot of people living in Charlemagne Ferron's first camp. They arrived in droves looking for work and were soon joined by their families. The time came when it was necessary to transform the little colony into a proper municipality, with a name, a mayor, a set of bylaws and municipal records. Ferron wanted a French name for the town, Byron Miles pushed for a Ukrainian one. But the lumberjacks had already taken to calling the place Sioux Junction, after the Indians who lived in the area and because of the two rivers that came together just north of the first encampment, the Wicked Sarah and the Belle River. Ferron wanted some farmers to settle in the area, and he wrote to the Quebec government, which sent him up a dozen colonists from the Beauce region. Soon he was no longer the only French speaker in Sioux Junction. His farmers spoke French, and Miles's lumberjacks—Rumanians, Irishmen and Germans—spoke a mixture of languages, mostly English, when they wanted to make themselves understood to each other.

There was never any trouble between Miles's men and Ferron's farmers. The anglophones, under the sway of Byron Miles—who was having less and less difficulty imitating the British accent of Sergeant Major Carruthers—lived on the west bank of the Belle River. The best agricultural land was to the east of the river, and it was there that Ferron, the first farmers from the Beauce and those that followed later established their farms. They grew mostly hay for fodder. Miles had paid back the bank and was dabbling in the gold market; six years after arriving in Sioux Junction he was a very rich man. He had long ago sent for Rhian, the beautiful Celt from Minnesota, and their marriage was the first one celebrated in Sioux Junction. Ferron, in his capacity as justice of the peace, conducted the wedding.

As the first colonist of Sioux Junction, Ferron became its first mayor and regional deputy, thereby concentrating in his person all the public offices—much like Jo Constant in more modern times. For his part, Miles busied himself developing the local economy. Power and prestige for Ferron; cash for Miles. As for little Obomsawin, she became fat and forgotten; eventually she left the town, leaving her four children behind. She no longer felt at home in Sioux Junction; she wanted to die alone, on the Sioux reserve that had recently been established farther north.

Other women came to the Junction, though. Nuns to look after the orphans—like Francis Obomsawin—and to set up schools for the settlers' children. Wives for the lumberjacks and farmers. To be followed, in time, by priests.

3

Obomsawin's case went to trial.

For a trial, you need a defendant, a judge, a Crown prosecutor, a defence lawyer, a jury, a court clerk, et cetera.

They know who the defendant is: Obom. And they have a clerk. Obviously it's Jo Constant, who is also Sioux Junction's mayor, sheriff, bailiff and justice of the peace. For a jury you need twelve people. The entire population of Sioux Junction numbers about thirty, if you don't count the two hundred Indians who live on the reserve, so there are enough to make a jury. That leaves a judge and two lawyers, who had to be brought in from outside. No problem. The provincial justice department will spring for that. Obomsawin is going to have a proper trial.

The judge is James H. Kendrick. A Toronto magistrate with a Supreme Court seat, for three months of the year he is also the itinerant judge for northwest Ontario, a region that stretches from Thunder Bay to the Manitoba border. He is presiding at Obomsawin's trial because he is bilingual, as are so many other ex-

Montreal anglophones who cut their political teeth in the Liberal Party.

The Crown prosecutor's name is Malcolm Lennox. He too is an itinerant; he is normally assigned to Ottawa, but once a year he makes excursions into the hinterland, usually in summer, when it suits him. Like Kendrick, Lennox is bilingual, which is why he's been given the case. He studied criminal law in Paris in his younger days, and then married a Québécoise. His French is impeccable.

The lawyer for the defence is Jack Fairfield. Fairfield is more than just bilingual: he's a full-fledged French-Canadian, originally from Nipissing; his father was a Beauchamp who had Anglicized his name for his children's sake, since it was so much easier to get ahead in life if you had an English name. The family had never been fully accepted by the anglos, however, and Jack Fairfield received almost all his education in French schools, except when he studied law in Toronto. He specializes in criminal law, and has his practice in Sudbury. He was chosen to represent Obomsawin and is being paid by legal aid, his client apparently not having a red cent to his name.

The three men arrive on the same float plane. This is the only way to get to Sioux Junction in a hurry: it's a tiny Cessna 440 operated by North Western Air Ontario, and normally it flies in only once a year, in the fall, with a load of Americans who come up to hunt bear. There is no other easy way in. The railroad track has been abandoned for at least ten years, and the forest road in from the main highway is almost impassable at the best of times, which this is not. It is also an easy road to get lost on, as Jo Constant had found out.

There being no landing strip at Sioux Junction, the pilot has to land on Lake Katibonka, about twenty miles from town. There's a small, rickety dock on the lake that still serves its purpose. Judge Kendrick has never been so far north before in his life. And he has never even heard of Sioux Junction. Neither have the two lawyers, but they don't say anything, just in case. In fact, the two lawyers have hardly opened their mouths during the whole trip: when they do speak, they address the judge. They are sizing each other up, getting to know each other. It's part of their job. They let the judge do the talking.

At the dock, Jo Constant is waiting for the judge in his rusty old station wagon. As sheriff, it's one of his duties to pick up the judge and bring him to the hotel. When he sees the two lawyers get out of the float plane, he offers to give them a lift for half the regular fare. He is also the town's only taxi driver. The lawyers shrug and get in; it all goes on the government's tab anyway.

At the wheel, Jo Constant is a happy man. For the first time since he reopened the hotel, he is making money. He plays up his role as host to the hilt, telling his passengers about the state of the forest, filling them in on the latest weather reports. The Crown attorney asks him something about Obomsawin, and Constant is about to reply when the defence lawyer stops him: it is against the rules, he says, to ask questions about the accused before the charges have been heard in court. The judge doesn't say anything; he is asleep, his head nodding up and down every time the station wagon hits a bump. The Crown attorney keeps quiet, too. This is going to be a long trial, he thinks to himself, if this nincompoop is going to be obsessed with procedure. Constant can't think of anything more to say. Everyone keeps quiet. They let the judge sleep.

Mme Constant welcomes everyone at the door of the Logdrivers Hotel. She came right out onto the step the moment she heard the station wagon pull up front. As fat as ever, she is wearing a bright orange dress and a white tablecloth that has never been used; after all, it isn't every day that a judge comes to stay at the Logdrivers Hotel.

At first, she is a bit ticked off with her husband; he could at least have opened the doors for his passengers. Jo, she sighs, just doesn't know how to do things proper. She says nothing, though, not wanting to cause a scene in front of the judge. She knows how to behave in public. But just you wait, you little bugger, she thinks; I'll get you later. When the three men get out of the car, she assumes that the judge is the one with the white hair, and she gives him her biggest, warmest smile: "Welcome, Your Honour!"

"You got the wrong one, my dear," her husband tells her. "The guy with the white hair's the defence lawyer, Mr. Fairfield."

"Get off my back, you idiot," she hisses. "Which one's the judge?"

"My very good wishes, madame," says the judge, stepping forward.

"My goodness, you don't look old enough to be a judge," says Cécile, flustered. "Who are these other two, then?"

When her husband explains the situation, Cécile snarls at him: "Why the hell didn't you tell me who all was coming? These guys are bigwigs too: where're we gonna put them, eh?"

Constant says they will manage. The two lawyers exchange smiles.

When you have to make do, you make do. According to Cécile, the only way they can manage is to evict the social worker—he's so doped up on antidepressants he won't notice anything anyway. They can kick Obomsawin out, too, for all she cares; after all, they can't very well house a criminal and a judge under the same roof, can they? At this point the defence lawyer observes that his client has yet to be convicted of any crime, and so cannot properly be called a criminal. The Crown attorney agrees. Jo says that they can work out the details after supper; the first thing to do is to get some food into these gents.

Jo is in good spirits. For the first time, the Logdrivers Hotel is turning people away. Things start to go downhill fairly quickly, though. The judge asks for a Scotch before dinner. The three of them are seated in the dining room, and the two lawyers are thirsty too.

The Crown attorney never touches liquor, he said, and orders a glass of orange juice. But the defence lawyer wants a dry martini on the rocks. "What are we going to do, Jo?"

Jo goes into the dining room and explains that he hasn't been in the hotel business very long, that he doesn't have much experience yet, they'll have to be a little patient with him, and so on. Mr. Fairfield smiles amicably and says he brought his own bottle of Scotch and he'd be glad to share it around. He is used to travelling in the boonies of northern Ontario, he says, and always carries his own supply. The judge accepts the offer, flinching under the disapproving glance of the Crown attorney.

Shortly after that a fourth customer arrives. This is a Mr. Latulippe, who lives more than three hundred kilometres south of Sioux Junction; he is one of the ones who saw Obomsawin's house burn down. Latulippe is a travelling salesman and comes up to the area quite often, but he has never stayed in the Logdrivers before. As the Crown's principal witness, however, he expects to be put up at the government's expense. Fine, but where? Jo asks himself.

Obviously, because he is a prisoner, Obom has to stay in the hotel. He can sleep in the Constants' apartment, on the fold-out sofa in the living room. The Great Depression doesn't want to go either; he paid for his room a year in advance, and as a good customer he has his rights. They can fix up a bed for him at night in the dining room. The witness will move into Obom's vacated room, along with the judge, and the two lawyers will share the Great Depression's room.

The lawyers are used to such measures, though, and don't grumble. The judge is somewhat less pleased; he'd been expecting a room to himself, but he recognizes that there isn't much choice. The trial won't last more than three days, anyway. When you have to make do, you make do.

The guests also want a bottle of wine with their supper; at least the judge and Mr. Fairfield do; they've already finished off the bottle of Scotch. Constant doesn't think it would be a good idea to tell them at this point that the hotel has lost its liquor licence—he's going to reapply pretty soon anyway, and no one will be any the wiser. And he knows where he can lay his hands on some wine. There is a bootlegger in town, old Kirkstead, who makes his own wine and beer and sometimes can be persuaded to part with it, for a price. Constant slips over to his place and buys six bottles of his best. Kirkstead has his own recipe: he pours a few pounds of Smyrna raisins into a garbage can full of water; when the raisins have swollen up to their original size, he squeezes them out in a presser, then adds a few bottles of 90 proof Alcool and some sugar. Two glasses of the resulting concoction are enough to put the most dedicated drinker under the table: local hunters always take a supply of it with them into the bush, and when they throw it up afterwards it's as black as pitch. New customers have certainly never tasted anything like it.

For supper, Mme Constant makes roast moose with baked potatoes and canned peas. The judge is surprised when he sees the hotel serving wild meat, since it's against the law in Canada, but he doesn't say anything because he loves game and hasn't had any for quite some time. He turns a blind eye and cleans his plate.

Constant is pouring wine for the first time in his life. His guests are put out a bit when they see that the bottles have no labels, but they keep quiet. Nothing up here is the same as anywhere else. The Crown attorney puts his hand over his glass and orders a Coke. Fairfield and Judge Kendrick make faces when they taste the wine, but they don't say anything: the wine list isn't exactly extensive. The witness, Latulippe, is the most contented; he's always been fond of Kirkstead's plonk.

After supper, the judge has a headache. He says good night and asks to be shown to his room. The witness is sound asleep in his chair. The two lawyers are talking about law school, their first trials, their future cases.

Suddenly, Obomsawin walks into the room. He has spent the whole day walking along the Wicked Sarah. Constant introduces him to the two lawyers, and Obom sits down with them and orders a meal and something to drink. They talk of this and that, without mentioning the upcoming trial. After a while a few other customers come in who have suddenly remembered that the Logdrivers is a hotel. They order drinks, and some of them even order food. In the kitchen, Cécile gets to work again and Jo goes back to the bootlegger's.

Things are going well, in other words. The Constants can't complain. They are in a bit of a rush to close for the night, though, because they have to get up early in the morning to make breakfast. But they'll manage, as Jo says. They're making money for once; why make things difficult?

They get through the night. All the guests go to bed, and Constant kicks the other customers out. The two lawyers go upstairs to their room, undress without looking at each other, get into their pyjamas and climb into their twin beds. There is only one problem: Fairfield warns his colleague that he always farts and snores in his sleep. At first, the Crown attorney wants to switch rooms and sleep with the judge, but he thinks it might look funny, so he changes his mind and says good night to Fairfield, who is already asleep. In the next room, the judge and the witness are sleeping back to back in the same bed, like a couple of babies.

Alone in the kitchen, Jo counts the cash: it's been a good day. Very good, in fact.

"Come to bed, Jo," Fat Cécile shouts down from their room. "We've got a lot of work to do tomorrow."

4

Obomsawin is alingual.

By which I mean he doesn't know any language very well, certainly not English or French. His first biographer wrote that Obom spoke nothing but Sioux throughout his childhood. His second biographer, not one to shy away from an exaggeration, asserted that the painter was fluent in four or five of the most important Indian dialects. We can now, however, set the record straight vis-à-vis Obomsawin and the Amerindian tongues: he didn't speak any of *them* very well. He knew one or two words of Sioux, Cree and Ojibway, but no more than any tourist who goes into northern Ontario and asks one of the few remaining natives: "How do you say, 'I'm hungry' or 'It's cold' in your language?" That's about all Obomsawin can say, I've asked him myself. He can understand a few dozen Sioux idioms, it's true, like most of the people in Sioux Junction who hang around with the Indians. But that is it.

But by saying he is alingual I'm referring only to his knowledge of English and French. And it isn't through ignorance; it's his choice.

Obviously he's closer to French culture than to English. He attended a French school when he was young, he spoke French all his life, and most of the books he read were in French. What's more, his mother, Flore Obomsawin, who worked as a cleaning lady in some of the posher homes in Sioux Junction, was a Frenchified half-breed. All of these are sufficient for more than a few of the town's francophones to claim Obomsawin as one of their own. To Obom himself, however, it doesn't amount to very much.

There are also those in town who take him for an anglophone. Wrongly, because his French background prevents him from becoming totally assimilated into English-speaking society. To him, English is never anything more than a useful language to know, a bit more useful than some of the other languages, maybe, but still just a tool. He speaks it easily, as do most Franco-Ontarians who have lived all their lives surrounded by a sea of English. And he can read and write it. But that's about as far as it goes. Put it this way: when he wants to read the instructions for some contest on the side of a box of cereal, he'll pick up the box and read without really being aware of whether he is looking at the French or the English side.

So he is neither French nor English. Through indifference, primarily, but also because he feels a certain amount of antipathy towards the two languages. Especially French. Very early in life he told himself that French was a "dangerous and degenerate" language. Oddly enough, it was the French teacher at his school who had taught him that. From the age of thirteen he simply refused to learn to speak French properly, rejected it with all the fervour of an adolescent having his first brush with the world of ideas; he made the decision calmly yet seriously, the way other children of his age decided they would never have children or join the armed forces. Disgusted by French, then, and ostracized by the natives, whose language he had never bothered to learn properly, he also steered clear of English, a language that he felt blurred and trivialized everything it tried to express. He preferred to remain alingual. His French was good enough—he occasionally uttered some clever phrases that he dredged up from God knows where—but he would be just as likely to spout long passages of grammarless English peppered with expressions in Sioux; at other times he would start to say something in English and end up in French, or the other way around. Never wholly one or the other. He now displays a regal disregard for the niceties of either: so what, *ça ne fait rien*. He is alingual.

I'm taking some time now to explain the relationship between Obom and the French language only because I find it interesting. Especially his statement that French is a "dangerous and degenerate" language. It certainly had never occurred to me to think of French in that way until I met Obomsawin. But now that I've become better acquainted with his former French teacher, and have even interviewed him a few times, I think I know exactly what he means.

The French teacher came to Sioux Junction when Obomsawin was very young; as a simple classroom instructor at first, but later he became the principal of Marie-du-Sacré-Coeur, the small separate school that Obomsawin attended. Even as principal, though, he continued to teach French, because he regarded all the other teachers in the school as incompetent. In fact, according to him, when it came to a proper understanding of the French language, the whole world was incompetent—except him.

His name was Monsieur Yelle, and he came from Ottawa. His own schooling, up to the bachelor of arts level, had been achieved with the aid of parish bursaries from the Oblate Fathers. When he graduated, he didn't have enough English—or enough contacts— to become a civil servant, so he went into teaching. He had the precise diction of those whose education has been strong on Greek and Latin, and he was fairly good-looking in his younger days. Sioux Junction was his first teaching post; he became principal of Marie-du-Sacré-Coeur a short time later, and stayed there for the next thirty years. All his children were born in Sioux Junction; he had married a local girl, and spent his entire life reminding her that he had come from Ottawa and she had come from Sioux Junction, and that he had had a classical education and she had not.

Because he spoke French so well—better, even, than the local priest—he quickly became an important person in Sioux Junction. He was M. Yelle, the French Master. Had he wanted to, he could have delivered the sermons on Sunday. All of his authority came from his mastery of the French language and from nowhere else, and it was this that he tried to instill in the young mind of Thomas Obomsawin, one of his most gifted pupils.

M. Yelle reigned supreme in a town where the chairman of the Separate School Board was an illiterate miner who held his hymnbook upside down in church. And where the parish priest had spent his entire life in lumber camps, and whose French had holes in it so big you could drive a logging truck through them; when he said Mass he pronounced the Latin words with a strong English accent, because he had completed his studies in Windsor, in southwestern Ontario. And where the rich were all self-made men who had never gone to school at all. The handsome young twenty-two-year-old schoolteacher had looked around him and quickly realized that he was the only person in town who could speak the language properly. Only he knew that the verb *réaliser* was an Anglicism; that you didn't say "the girl I'm going out with," but "the young lady with whom I'm going out," or better yet, "the light of my life"; that it was wrong to say "hopefully" when you meant "one hopes that ...." Et cetera, et cetera. The young French master laid into the town's citizens mercilessly, correcting their grammar with a kind of dia-bolical delight. People began to be afraid to open their mouths when he was around; he knew that, and revelled in his superiority.

M. Yelle is still remembered in Sioux Junction. In the summer, he used to promenade along the streets, dressed always in a black suit with a fake carnation in his buttonhole, cane in hand and a spotless Panama hat on his head. The great professor of disdain for all those who abused the French language, the guardian of a mystical treasure of grammatical illogicalities, verbose pedanticisms and perfectly incomprehensible metaphors. He alone could be counted on to utter such phrases as: "I have a weakness for champagne, the very king of the French vineyards," with all the savoir-faire of a life member of the French Academy. And he could pull it off, too: no one laughed at him. People respected his knowledge, especially since no one knew any better, as it were. He was quite a sight, waving his cane in front of people as he favoured them with a few well-chosen (and carefully rehearsed) bon mots; he made people ashamed of their own way of speaking, made them search too hard for just the right phrase. He would fix them with a malignant regard, then continue on his way, casting his pearls of conversation as he went, caressing his artificial boutonnière. Even Roland Provençal was afraid of him.

M. Yelle noticed Thomas Obomsawin quite early on: the youngster expressed himself well, learned quickly and seemed to have a special aptitude for drawing. All the same, he says now, he remembers telling himself at the time that the poor little tyke was never going to amount to much in the world because he didn't come from a good family, he didn't have any money to speak of and he was often seen in disreputable company.

Today, M. Yelle is retired and living in St. Petersburg, Florida. But he remembers Obomsawin very well. In the thirty-five years he spent in Sioux Junction, he says, he never had more than five or six good students. Little Carmen Richer, whose father was the mayor and a millionaire; Pierre Carrière, who is now in the foreign service; a handful of others, and Obomsawin, who became a famous painter and who must be close to fifty by now. M. Yelle remembers them all. Carmen and Pierre were very good in French; they even went together to the provincial competitions. Carmen won first prize in diction; Pierre, who came from a poor but hardworking family, swept up all the other prizes, the most prestigious of which had been a bursary to attend the Jesuit College in Sudbury—a classical education, and all expenses paid! "That Pierre Carrière, my young friend, he was my pride and joy," M. Yelle says today. "Imagine: eight years of first-class schooling, all free—lodging, meals, laundry. And after that he went on to acquire his master's degree at Laval University in Quebec, still on a bursary from the Jesuits. And even that was not all: from there he went to Paris, to the Sorbonne, thanks to which he was able to enter the diplomatic corps. All because he was good enough in the French language to succeed at the provincial competitions! I did right to encourage him! I don't hear from him very often any more, but I gather he is quite highly placed in External Affairs. An ambassador, I believe, or something along those lines. And he owes everything, my dear sir, to the fact that he spoke French well when he was young, and that he took my advice. Obomsawin could have done every bit as well, but he wouldn't listen to me. Pierre has even married a young woman from a wealthy family, and they have beautiful children who are attending a real French lycée. Not bad for the son of a lumberjack who worked at the Sauvé brothers' sawmill ...."

M. Yelle had always believed that if you were good in French you would have no trouble making your way through life. Having respect for the language was not just a way of showing that you had respect for yourself; it was a way of making others respect you. "And when they respect you, they'll fear you, they'll always think you more intelligent than you really are. And that opens all kinds of doors: just look at what happened to Pierre Carrière from Sioux Junction."

"Tell me, M. Yelle," I asked him. "Can you name any other French-Canadian kids who have succeeded in life as much as Pierre Carrière?"

"No one. No one else. He's the only one."

"One kid in the whole town?"

"That's right."

"What about Obomsawin?"

"Little Obom? Well, I can't speak for his paintings—I've never seen them. I hear he's sold quite a few of them, that he's made lots of money from them, but that he's spent it all, as all artists do. He ought to have worked to solidify his reputation, while continuing to paint, earning his money over the long term instead of all at once, then invested it wisely so he could live off the revenue in Florida. As I've done. Obom never listened to anyone. He never wanted to hear anything from me."

"What would you have told him?"

M. Yelle launched into his favourite theme, always the same: the only way for a French-Canadian to succeed in life was to master the French language. Absolutely the only way. Even Obomsawin still remembers the advice he received from M. Yelle.

The French teacher had done everything he could to change the young Thomas Obomsawin, to get him off on the right foot. He had him over to his house in the evenings, and talked to him for hours in a little study he had fixed up, separated from the rest of the house; and as he talked—to himself, half the time—he would pour himself shot glasses of alcool, cheap whiskey that would eventually make him forget his education, forget even his beloved language. "Obom," he would say (Obom would be about thirteen years old at this time), "Obom, try to talk like a Frenchman, like a real French-

man from France. Enunciate every syllable, like I do in the classroom; people are so stupid, don't pay any attention to them if you
make a mistake. Just go on. And don't say, 'Where's my mitts?' Say,
'Has anyone seen my gloves?' Always use unusual words, long
words, words that no one else will understand: you'll be surprised
how impressed people are by things they don't understand. Do like
I say, Obom, and you'll never go wrong."

(These little private sessions served as a pretext for M. Yelle to
get drunk. He would make a lot of grammatical errors during
them—sometimes on purpose.)

"Obom, never use English words if you can help it; always use
good French words instead. It throws people off, lets 'em know that
you know what's what. And stop calling yourself Tom, or Obom;
make people call you Thomas. You should probably consider
changing your family name altogether. But choose a real French
name—not a stupid local one, like Girard or Tremblay, but a real
good name from somewhere else. People will notice it, they'll
remember it.

"Listen carefully to what I'm telling you, my young friend: in
France, eh, the French want everyone to speak like them. It's the
only way. If you go there and talk to them the way you talk around
here, they'll write you off as some kind of country hick, it don't
matter if you're a mathematical genius, they won't have nothing to
do with you. No way. Not even if you're a millionaire! I'm just telling
you so's you'll know: if you're ever in France, speak good French,
eh? They'll respect you. And when you come back to Canada?
Whuff! The whole world will spread itself out at your feet. I'm
serious! You won't even have to go to school—everyone will think
you've been there already! Just speak good French, Tom, that's all
you need to do. Absolutely all.

"Look at me, Obom. Model yourself after me. Everyone in
Sioux Junction respects me. They all call me Monsieur Yelle. No one

ever calls me by my first name. The priest doesn't dare contradict me because he knows I can talk rings around him, I can bury him alive in six sentences. And all the rich guys in town ask my advice on a whole bunch of stuff. Because I express myself well. They come to me and ask me to write letters for them. Important letters! I write speeches for our Member of Parliament, who is just an uneducated French-Canadian slob with a lot of money. When he gives a speech in his awful stupid rural pea-soup accent, it's my words that everyone hears. When he stands up in the House of Commons, it's me who's speaking to the whole country. Can you even *imagine* the power that gives me? Eh? Even the English in Sioux Junction respect me, because they know people listen to me. They think I'm intelligent and—and cultivated, because I talk like them. All this because I speak good French, Obom."

I don't know how often Obom was subjected to M. Yelle's call for the domination of others through the power of the French language, but I do know that he was never interested in playing that game. It sickened him, he told me later, to have to hide his own language in order to impress other people. He also could have done what so many others before and after him have done—passed over into English. But he didn't want to switch, either. As he put it: "When I speak English, you could sort of say that others are speaking for me. I somehow feel that I'm not myself."

Neither one nor the other. Obom prefers to keep his distance from all languages; when he has to speak at all, he uses a form of French that is probably closer to Cajun. His alingualism has served him well, it must be said: what use does he have for language, anyway, when he has his painting?

5

Obomsawin has never loved anyone.

No one. Not even his mother. Flore Obomsawin did every-thing she could think of to make him love her, but her caresses and tender words never drew the slightest response from her son. In love, Thomas was as lucky as an alley cat: he went to this one when he was hungry, that one when he wanted stroking, and he left them all without a word of thanks. Even as a baby, his mother told me, he never cried; he demanded things, and when he got them he never said another word. And he never liked to be picked up.

The general feeling about Flore Obomsawin is that she did what she could for Thomas, that she tried as hard as she was able, but that circumstances were against her. She could never give him a normal childhood. When she first became pregnant with him, the priest forbade her to come back to Mass. She was, after all, a fallen woman. She had no business going to church if she was going to celebrate Easter before Palm Sunday! In spite of everything, though, there were some kind souls in the parish; Dr. Camirand, for example, who wanted Flore to give the baby up for adoption. She was healthy, intelligent and, as he put it, less savage than most of her race—any family would be happy to take her baby off her hands. A couple of young professionals in Toronto, for instance, people with money who could give the child a good upbringing, a good education. Flore was called heartless when she refused these kind offers. She wanted to keep her baby.

She suffered for it. It seemed the whole world wanted her to give her child up. The Sioux living on the reserve, for instance, wanted the baby, who would be one of their race. Flore had the right to move to the reserve and raise her child there, but she wouldn't hear of it: why live on the reserve when she had a fine house in Sioux Junction, where she could earn her own living? She didn't want to owe anything to anyone.

After the Sioux, it was the Children's Aid Society's turn. The CAS wanted to place her child with "a responsible family." For the child's own good, you understand. An unwed mother couldn't possibly raise a baby properly, and when you think of all the childless couples who were unable to have children of their own .... Sioux Junction's resident social worker made countless visits to Flore's home, trying to talk her out of her baby. Flore was adamant: she kept her hands folded across her swollen belly and said not a word.

In the end, Flore won out. When her contractions started, she went to stay with a childhood friend who lived on a farm not far from Sioux Junction. Dr. Camirand delivered the baby, but he agreed to keep quiet about it. After three months, Flore returned to her house in town, the one her father had left her, carrying her young son in a wicker basket. It was too late for the Children's Aid Society—the regulatory adoption period had passed. The Sioux had no rights over the child, because he hadn't been born on the reserve. Flore had thumbed her nose at everyone.

She lived very happily with her little Thomas for quite some time. She raised him as best she could, hiring herself out as a cleaning lady here and there, leaving Thomas with friends when she had to go to work. It wasn't easy, of course; there were plenty of people in town who wouldn't speak to her because she was an unwed mother. But she stood up to them: "As long as they let me do what I have to do," she said, "they can say what they like."

The day came, however, when Flore had had enough of living on her own. A little rent money wouldn't hurt, she told herself, and it would be good for Tom to have a man around the house. She took in a lodger, a mine worker who had come to Sioux Junction after losing his job in Sudbury. The man's name was Bob; he was married with children, but his family had stayed behind. Bob was a restless man, and before long he was making advances to Flore, who for her part wasn't averse to having a man of her own. Everything went well at first. She was a good cook, kept a tidy house, knew how to give a man pleasure; he was kind and considerate, liked to do odd jobs, didn't drink too much. But it didn't last. Before long, Bob lost his job because he was always arriving late for work; he took to drinking and beating up on Flore; he stopped paying rent and hung around the house all day doing nothing. The neighbours would often hear the two of them fighting; Bob would storm out in the middle of the night, and come back the next morning begging Flore to give him another chance. And she would. Once, though, he hit her a little too hard, and Chief Crozier, the head of Sioux Junction's police force, paid him a visit and taught him a few things about cohabitation. The next day, Bob left town.

The incident spurred the Children's Aid Society to renew its attack, and this time it was determined not to miss such a golden opportunity. Flore was told she was not raising her son like everyone else, that she would lose him if she didn't change her lifestyle. Little Thomas seemed to be growing up at the normal rate: he was walking by the age of one; he was toilet trained at two; by three, he was talking a mile a minute. Flore couldn't see what she was doing wrong.

But her luck couldn't hold. Thomas was around six when Bob left. Not long after that, Flore was raped by three drunk men at the reserve. She had to be taken to the hospital in Thunder Bay, because her attackers had beaten her pretty badly, and once there she sank into a kind of depression. She didn't speak a word, just lay in her bed smoking cigarettes all day, watching television for hours on end. She didn't even speak when the CAS took her son away, and when she recovered, she was not allowed to see him. They had won. Flore sank into a second depression, deeper than the first. She was saved from this state by a man who worked at the Sauvé brothers' sawmill, a young fellow named Larry who loved her to distraction. Larry wasn't always playing with a full deck, but he was honest and hard-working and a good sort. He even wanted to have children, but Flore was no longer capable of that.

Flore did everything she could to find out what had happened to her son, Thomas. The Children's Aid Society would tell her nothing, except that she would never see him again. She might as well get used to the idea, they said, tell herself that her son was dead and gone to the Happy Hunting Ground of Adopted Children.

Meanwhile, Thomas was in the United States. It's a long story, but in those days the regional offices of the Children's Aid Society were under steady pressure to place cute little Indian kids with families in the United States. The theory was that they would be too hard to raise if they were placed close to their native woods and reserves; they would run away and commit atrocious crimes. And it's true that as soon as they were old enough, a lot of Indian children did slip away from their adoptive families and return to the land of their birth; after that they were very difficult to recapture, and their adoptive families were put to a lot of trouble. At that time the social worker for the Sioux Junction region was an old battle-ax named Miss Van Schellenberger, a Mormon, who believed with all her might that her little Indian children were much better off being sent to large cities, somewhere completely different from the lives they were used to. The farther away, the more surrounded by concrete, the better; places where there were good, white, Christian families who would help the children forget their savage backgrounds, their miserable pasts. Such places were usually found in the United States.

It so happened that Miss Van Schellenberger had a cousin in Chicago, who was also Mormon, and also a social worker. This cousin ran a Mormon mission in Africa that was constantly short of money. To help finance the mission, she undertook from time to time to find children for couples who were unable to have families of their own. Proper adoption procedures took so much time, and were so expensive, and so complicated, and even then were never sure. Miss Van Schellenberger's cousin could come up with children as if by magic; in exchange, she would accept small donations for her work in Africa. Every now and then, accordingly, she would get into her car and drive to Canada, and return with one or two little Indian children that no one wanted, so she said, and who would be so happy to live with good Christian families in the Chicago area. And that's how young Thomas Obomsawin disappeared from Sioux Junction one day, and found himself living in Skokie, Illinois, the next.

This is no fairy tale: it still happens today, Indian children from Saskatchewan and Manitoba sent to the United States for adoption. It makes for fewer criminals in Canada, and American families—which are having more and more trouble finding suitable children to adopt—get a steady supply of cute ethnic kids. But it doesn't always work out so cozily. Some children, whether installed in

Arizona or in the heart of New Jersey, never stop trying to run away and return to their original homes. Many succeed. So it was that young Thomas Obomsawin turned up one fine morning in Sioux Junction, after having been away for three years. Everyone in town was amazed! Flore's neighbours all wanted to know what had happened to him, why he had run away. Children's Aid was furious, of course, and tried to send him back, but Flore was having none of that this time, no sir .... She hired a lawyer, on the advice of her live-in friend, Larry, and the lawyer wrote a menacing letter to Miss Van Schellenberger who, it should be noted, had been accepting small commissions from her cousin in Chicago to fund her own Mormon interests. There was no more trouble from Children's Aid. Flore was finally convinced that her little Thomas had been returned to her forever. A beautiful child who had saved himself from a terrible fate and come home to his true mother—he must be an angel! She welcomed him like a prince! The homecoming scene is still etched in Obomsawin's mind today; it's the most vivid memory of his entire life.

He is standing in his mother's kitchen. A pot of cabbage and beef is simmering on the stove, and the smell fills the room. He is wearing his Sunday clothes but they are filthy, and he has a notebook full of drawings under his arm. Neighbours are gathered around, staring at him as if he had just landed from the planet Mars. He understands maybe half of the French words they are flinging at him: How is he feeling? Is he hungry? He looks so pale! He understands all the English words, but he doesn't answer a single question put to him in that language: it would make him feel he hadn't run away far enough. His mother is beside herself with joy; she hugs him over and over again, asking him if he is really her lost son come back to her after all these years. All her odours are familiar to him: her breath still smells of candies and tobacco; her armpits reek of hard work. Her hair is blonde now—she has taken to dyeing it, he learns later, to make herself look less Indian and because Larry likes blondes. Tom has to look closely at her a few times to make sure it's really her. Standing beside her is a tall stranger with a brush cut and huge ears; he laughs and talks very loudly, and is continually handing out bottles of beer to the other adults. His name is Larry, and he's his mother's boyfriend. He seems a nice guy. When everyone else leaves, Larry stays. "Jesus Christ, boy," he says to him, "what kinda hell'd you go through to get yourself back here?"

Thomas kept the story to himself for a long time. He was still afraid that they would send him back; if they knew how he had made his escape, they would surely take measures to prevent him from repeating his exploits—maybe even place him in a detention centre. In the States, he had learned how to keep his mouth shut in order to protect himself—it was a lesson that would stay with him all his life.

But he never forgot what had happened to him in Chicago. He spoke to me about it much later—as his third biographer—when he was no longer afraid of being locked up or sent back. He had been placed with a good family. The father worked and the mother stayed home. He was their only child, and he went to school every day and they made him take a bath every night. He didn't eat much for a boy of his age, and they discovered that he had bad teeth. After that he went to the dentist every two weeks. They spoke English to him all the time, and he understood most of what they said. But when he cried he spoke French, and the other children in the neighbourhood laughed at him because they didn't understand what he was saying.

The very first book they gave him when he learned how to read was the story of a small boy named Johnny who ran away from home because his parents were wicked and he wanted to see the world. Johnny saved up enough money for the trip by doing little odd jobs for the old ladies in his neighbourhood; then, when he had enough, he tied up a few belongings in a bundle—a change of clothes, his piggy bank, some cheese, nuts, carrots and raisins—and made his escape. He had also put his teddy bear in the bundle. Thomas remembers reading this book every night before going to bed; he kept it hidden in the garage. Then, one day, he too packed up and took off. In the book, Johnny's parents hardly noticed he was gone. He travelled around the world—Spain, Africa, China, Brazil—and ended up finding his true parents. Nine-year-old Thomas did the same thing, although he didn't see as much of the world. He didn't have that much money in his purse.

6

Sioux Junction shares a tradition with several other northern
Ontario towns.

Although this tradition doesn't have a name, the ritual is the
same everywhere: the townspeople roll an old, used car—usually a
wreck that has seen its last days—out onto the ice in the middle of
the lake, sometime early in the new year. The choice of car is very
important. It's made after Twelfth Night; everyone vies for the
honour of donating their favourite old heaps for the sacrifice. They
stand up one by one and extol their champion's virtues: the mileage
it has given them, the accidents it survived, how much (or how little)
they paid for it, et cetera. This all takes place at a huge bingo party
held in the parish hall on the first Saturday after Epiphany; a vote
is taken, there's plenty of laughter, a few bottles are passed around,
someone plays some music. Everyone has a good time.

The following Saturday, the chosen vehicle is pushed out onto
the lake, which of course is frozen solid. This is the first part of the
ritual, and is the responsibility of the youths of the town—the

strongest and loudest of them, at any rate. The others follow as the leaders plow the wreck through the snow from the municipal dump, singing songs, laughing, playing tricks on one another, tumbling into snow banks. Sometimes, for a joke, the prettiest girls in town are hoisted onto the wreck to make it heavier, and those pushing it have to push harder. The leaders curse, the girls laugh, small children start out lending a hand, then climb into the wreck themselves through the broken windows—they'll have their turn another year.

In Sioux Junction, this ritual always takes place on Lake Winnissogan because it's as deep as the ocean and already contains a whole dumpfull of old cars. It's choked with weeds, no good for fishing except in winter. And no one has drowned in it, so no one is offended by the shenanigans.

When the car arrives at the lake, the rest of the town is already there waiting for it. The exhausted youths relinquish their places to the stronger of the townspeople—not just to the men, either, for some of the women are easily as strong as their husbands. Everyone joins in and pushes the wreck out to the exact middle of the lake.

And then the party starts. People want to be photographed standing beside the wreck. Someone makes rude drawings on the doors, or writes things on the ice like "Rita loves John" or "Ti-Coune Gagnon wets his bed" and so on. There is merrymaking all around the wreck, everyone saying anything that comes into their heads and no one taking charge: they've come to have fun, not to listen to a bunch of official speeches. Afterwards there are some organized sports—ice-fishing derbies, with a prize for the biggest fish; skidoo races; tug-o'-wars; strongman contests, when the lumberjacks toss huge poles into the air; strongwoman contests. Fires are started on the ice to heat up the huge pots of pork and beans and venison stew; one cauldron is reserved for cooking up a big mess of moose, beaver, bear, partridge and rabbit, according to the time-honoured recipe set down by old Lucien Charron of Sturgeon Falls—greasy as hell, but it sticks to your ribs and tastes wonderful. The pork and beans are also out of this world, you don't want to miss that. Homemade wine kept at forty degrees Fahrenheit that knocks you flat after three mouthfuls, bootleg liquor that'll kill you if you have too much of it, cheap brandy, bottles of rye. Not much beer, because it would freeze. Everyone has a mickey of something in their pocket, and they pass it around in exchange for a gulp of someone else's. The kids drink as much Coke and lemonade as they can before it freezes. For dessert there's always hot raisin pie, molasses pie, doughnuts and coffee.

There are accidents, sometimes. These things happen. A skidoo will tip over, one of the children may be hurt while pushing the wreck, someone who has had too much to drink will fall into a fire. Fights break out, too, but there are always plenty of people around to stop them. Almost everyone has fond memories of the tradition—the proof of which is that it's still going on to this day, although not in Sioux Junction.

Some of the young people have been known to take advantage of the occasion to, shall we say, get to know each other better. Afterwards, they usually get married and have children. For many of them, the Festival of the Wreck is remembered as the day of their first kiss, or the first time they made love. Obom remembers the custom well—for him, it was the day of his first girl and his first kiss, both at the same time.

The most important event at the Festival of the Wreck, however, is the placing of bets, because that is, after all, the whole point of the affair. When the dented-up old wreck is placed in the middle of the lake, everyone tries to predict the exact date in the spring when the ice will be thin enough for it to fall through. In this way, they are in fact predicting the first day of summer; it happens in May, usually, or sometimes June, because summer can come damned late up here. People bet about a dollar; no more, because it's supposed to be all in fun. And whoever picks the right day usually splits the pot anyway, and if the weather is fine they throw another party to celebrate the return of summer.

The placing of bets is accompanied by the most nonsensical proceedings imaginable: everyone wants to know how much the car weighs, they consult almanacs, they base their predictions on the screwiest of theories. And everyone gives an explanation for their choice of dates: "I'll take May 15th because that's the day I lost my cherry!" The crowd laughs: someone always came up with that one. "I'll take June the 2nd, it's my wedding anniversary," to which her husband replies: "No, by the jeez, that's not your lucky day!" And everyone laughs again. Pretty soon everyone gets into the swing of it, especially when they begin to feel a bit tipsy. It isn't all laughs, though; there are serious moments, too. Like when one woman came up and said: "I bet the car will sink through the ice on June 14th," and everyone looked at her and remembered that that was the day she had lost her youngest son in a hunting accident. A couple of people gave her a hug, and nobody said anything.

Obomsawin placed a bet only once, just for a laugh. He picked June 17. He called it out loudly, even though he was standing next to the barrel where the men were taking bets. Afterwards, a girl came up to speak to him. It was young Carmen Richer; she was very good-looking, petite, pleasantly muscular and full of life, according to her friends at the convent. And she had the only green eyes in Sioux Junction. Her teeth were as straight and white as sugar cubes.

"Thomas," she said, "tell me why you chose June 17."

"Why do you want to know?"

"Because that's the day I come back from the convent for the summer. I was just wondering, that's all."

"I didn't have a reason before," said Thomas. "But I do now."

In point of fact, Carmen Richer shouldn't have been at the

festival at all. Traditionally, the party was off-limits to the town's gentry: those with money to burn would say what a shame it was to waste an old wreck like that when someone could have towed it to the scrap-metal yard and made a few bucks from it. The parish priest stayed away, too: he had once been asked to come and bless the sacrificial chariot, and had nearly strangled the person who had done the asking. So it had become a kind of pagan festival. Luckily, since without the representatives of church and state the people could have twice as much fun. It was a bit rowdy, especially for the younger generation who weren't used to drinking hard liquor; and for the Indians who would somehow always be involved when the fighting started; and for the teenagers, who would come to the party and sneak off into the woods to get into things they shouldn't—such as each other. According to the woman who kept house for the parish priest, there were even a couple of young girls who had become pregnant at the festival after making love fully clothed, lying down in the snow. All of which meant that Carmen Richer, who had just turned fifteen, was a little bit out of her element. If her parents had known she was there, there would have been the devil to pay.

Although she knew the party was no place for a girl from the convent, she didn't really care. She was like her father: she always did what she had a mind to do. Going up to Tom Obomsawin and speaking to him was a case in point. Why did she do it? No one knew very much about him at that time, whether he was going to turn out good or bad. No one even knew who his father was. What they did know was that he had just spent three years in a reform school, and they could surmise a lot from that. But Carmen had gone up to speak to him because she had felt like it, and her father could go piss up a rope!

And she had just said a few words to him, that was all. At least for the time being. Later, when the party was in full swing around two o'clock in the afternoon, after everyone had congratulated the winner of the skidoo race, Thomas had gone looking for her to resume the conversation. He found her with a group of friends, but they all cleared off when he approached and left the two alone. Thomas and Carmen sat down behind one of the ice-fishing huts and talked for the better part of an hour. At one point, when they felt cold, Carmen took a couple of slugs from Thomas's mickey of rum: she nearly gagged, but she said she felt warmer. Tom told her about the things he wanted to do; she told him she was leaving the next day for the convent. "Will you be in town this summer?" Neither of them could remember who had asked the question, but both of them remember saying "Yes" at the same time.

A short distance from the ice-fishing hut someone had scratched "Thomas loves Carmen" in the ice with a sharp stick, and drawn a heart around the words with an arrow through it and the date. When she saw it, Carmen began to laugh; Thomas didn't seem to find it so funny. "Oh, come on, Tom," she chided him. "It's just something written on the ice ..."

The next day, in church, the parish priest delivered a sermon against the evils of drink: half the congregation was suffering from a hangover and regretting the excesses of the day before. Carmen had already left for the convent in Sturgeon Falls—there was no high school in Sioux Junction—and Thomas was out looking for a job to pay for the canvas, brushes and paints that he needed. She wouldn't be home very often—Christmas, Easter and two months in the summer, that was it. You'd best forget all about her, Obom told himself.

That year Obom won the bet: the wreck disappeared into the lake on June 17. The lucky stiff. With his winnings he bought himself a pair of white duck trousers and a leather jacket, and he looked like a million dollars. He wanted to look sharp for Carmen when she returned from the convent.

He saw her again that summer, and they started going steady—

on the sly, of course. Although it was difficult, if not impossible, for anything to be going on on the sly in a town as small as Sioux Junction, no one seemed to suspect that they were seeing each other. Her parents certainly didn't know about it: if they did, Carmen's father was more than capable of beating the tar out of little sixteen-year-old Obomsawin, and her mother was equally capable of locking Carmen up in a convent and throwing away the key.

No one even remembered that some joker had written "Thomas loves Carmen" in the ice on a frozen lake. After all, it's not as if it was carved in stone.

That was also the year Thomas got his first job—working for the Sauvé Brothers. First in the cutting plant at the Upper Mill, then driving logs in the spring, and then at the big sawmill outside town for the summer. When Carmen came home for Easter vacation and saw the logs floating down the Wicked Sarah, she knew that the lumberjacks themselves would soon follow as they changed camps to keep up with the drive. As more logs appeared, piling up in huge jams at each river bend, she knew her Tom was coming closer and closer to her. Soon the river was completely choked, and the badly lit side streets of Sioux Junction came alive in the evenings with lumberjacks hurrying after their wives and children. Thomas got into town just in time for St.-John-the-Baptist Day, and Carmen felt herself the luckiest girl in the world. When the men climbed out of the riverboat, hers was among them.

7

In the old days there was also a music teacher in Sioux Junction. It was indirectly through him that Obomsawin came into the world.

Properly speaking, he wasn't a real music teacher, with a diploma or anything. He was self-taught. During the day he worked at the mine as a chemist; at night he practised his music. As he got older, the music became more and more important to him. His job as a chemist was just a way of putting food on the table.

His name was Omer Grandmaître, and he was a fine fellow in every sense of the term. He was fine as silk—he wouldn't hurt a fly. He was well liked by everyone in town, and if hardly anyone went to his funeral a few years ago it was because there was hardly anyone still living in Sioux Junction by then. Omer was one of the few who had wanted to stay.

There had been music in Sioux Junction before Omer Grandmaître, of course. Obomsawin's great-grandmother used to sing Sioux lullabies to her children, and almost everyone had some form of music. The French-Canadian lumberjacks and farmers had their fiddlers among them, as well as other entertainers who could make music and songs out of just about anything: handsaws that could be made to wail like banshees; homemade squeeze boxes; jew's-harps; accordions; flutes for the ladies. The Scots and Bretons who had come to work in the woods and, later, in the mines for Byron Miles, brought along their bagpipes; the Ukrainians, with their powerful voices, sang the haunting songs of their homeland and danced with all the abandon of soldiers on the eve of a great battle. Since there was little else to do in Sioux Junction in the evenings, everyone took to learning the songs, music and dances of everyone else, so that eventually there were Québécois who could play the bagpipes as well as any clansman, Finnish fiddlers and Ukrainians who could dance a mean jig.

The first organ arrived in Sioux Junction three years before the town had its first priest. After that the Ukrainian Catholics had to have one of their own, bigger and better than the first. Then the Anglicans decided they couldn't live without one.

As the town prospered, the wealthier citizens found they could afford pianos. The first piano to be delivered to Sioux Junction was for the Sauvés, the family that owned the sawmill. Old Raymond Sauvé had a heart of flint, but he loved music. His wife taught herself to play, and a year later was holding concerts in her salon. Sioux Junction's horizons were expanding. In ten years, there was one piano for every three families. It would be an exaggeration to say that everyone in town played the piano, but just about everyone who had a good bank account owned one. Soon the children were tinkling away at the ivories and nearly everyone had a piano in the house to put trophies, knickknacks and photographs on.

M. Grandmaître had been born in Saint-Ours-sur-Richelieu, the same village in Quebec as Charlemagne Ferron, Sioux Junction's founder. He had studied chemistry at the University of Montreal, then almost immediately took a job in Sioux Junction in order to make a lot of money in a hurry and then move back to Montreal to get married. He made the money, all right, but he never went back. He kept his job at the mine until his death, even when everyone else had moved away. He said he felt needed and liked here.

And he was. With everyone buying pianos and every other kind of musical instrument as if they were going out of style, M. Grandmaître grew more and more in demand. He had studied a bit of music at the Montreal Conservatory when he had been a university student; he knew how to read music and was the only one in town who could teach it properly. So every evening he would leave work and hurry home to an incredibly busy schedule. Monday nights were practice nights for the Melomaniacs, a subgroup of the French Choral Society; Tuesday nights he gave lessons to the more gifted students in town (those who could afford to pay did; for those who couldn't, the lessons were free); Wednesdays he directed the English choral group, Sioux Junction's Music Lovers. Thursday he directed again, either the chamber music quartet put together by Mrs. Bertrand, an embalmer at the local funeral parlour, or else Lyric Theatre North, which had been rehearsing an operetta by Offenbach, no less, for the past two years. Fridays he accompanied the pianist at the silent-movie house on the violin; Saturday it was a whole slew of things; Sunday he played the organ in three separate churches: the hours of service for all three—the French Catholic cathedral, the Ukrainian Catholic church and the Anglican temple— were regulated according to Omer's frantic timetable. If he had wanted to, Omer could easily have made a good living from his music alone, but he refused to quit his job at the mine because he had a low opinion of his own musical ability. "If I had as much talent as I have energy," he would say, "I'd be playing at Carnegie Hall, not at the Marie-du-Sacré-Couer parish hall in Sioux Junction, Ontario."

One day Omer collapsed at work from sheer physical exhaustion. For three weeks there was almost no music in town. After that, Omer realized that he couldn't go on doing everything himself, and he began to look around for an assistant.

He soon found one in the form of a handsome young man of twenty-five named Christos Sperdouklis, who was working as a kitchen helper in one of the Sauvé brothers' lumber camps. The workers at the camp called him Figaro, because when he rolled out his pie dough he would always be singing operatic arias. There was one in particular that everyone liked, and one day someone asked him what it was called: Christos explained that it was from *The Marriage of Figaro*, an opera written by some Austrian composer named Mozart about a barber who could sing. The name stuck because Christos also used to cut hair in the camp in the evenings and because, well, between you and me, Figaro is a lot easier to say than Christos Sperdouklis.

It turned out that Figaro could do just about anything he set his mind to, and do it well. He could bake pies, sew on buttons, repair engines that broke down for no reason at all, get radios going that hadn't worked for ages, fix watches, grow flowers in half a square inch of poor soil. And he had the devil's own luck in hunting and fishing and at cards.

As a result, he was well liked in camp. Even with his fifty words of English and thirty words of French, he could talk all night long about just about anything. He never played a dirty trick on anyone, and his kitchen was always as clean as an operating room. And he had another rare quality: handsome as he was, he never fooled around with the other lumberjacks' wives or girlfriends. He knew how to bide his time.

After a while, though, Figaro began to tire of camp life. He wanted to see something of the world, to spend some of the money he had saved up. When the cook at the Sauvé brothers' plant in Sioux Junction quit one day, Figaro applied for the job immediately and was transferred from the Upper Camp. And that's how Christos, the silver-tongued Figaro, came down to Sioux Junction.

It didn't take Omer Grandmaître long to notice him: the little Greek had a beautiful voice and an almost perfect ear. On his days off, instead of going out drinking and chasing women with the rest of the men from the sawmill, Christos would go to Omer's house and learn how to repair musical instruments. Omer had about fifty of them by this time: all the strings, all the winds, all the woods, two pianos, an organ, even a harpsichord. He also had quite a few rare or antique instruments that he had had sent over from Europe. Whenever he had a few dollars set aside, he'd spend it on musical instruments or opera scores. (No wonder he died naked in a museum, as Roland Provençal would say after his death.)

After a year, Figaro could play anything. He liked the guitar and the piano best, but nothing daunted him: it quickly became apparent that Figaro was the best student Omer had ever had.

The town had nothing to reproach him for, either. Well, maybe one little thing: he never went to Mass. But he was excused for that; he was probably Greek Orthodox, people said, and there was no Greek Orthodox church in Sioux Junction. There were also suggestions ... nothing malicious, mind you ... that for a young man as handsome as he was, well, he must have been popular with the girls. When he spoke about his past he said he had come from the old country, that he had seen the Holy Land as a child, and Egypt; as for the future, he said he'd like to marry a girl from his homeland and open up a restaurant. And the director of the local credit union let it slip out one day that Christos's bank account was fairly hefty: he always deposited his entire pay cheque, minus deductions.

In any case, it was Christos who began helping Omer in his duties as the music master of Sioux Junction. It began innocently enough—repairing broken strings, tuning the pianos—but before long he was directing the choral society and the chamber music quartet, and doing every bit as good a job as Omer had done. And as it turned out, he did have quite a way with women. More so than anyone had thought. When it came to teaching the ladies how to sing, it was said, Christos really knew the score.

He was careful, though. No one suspected that he was sleeping with Dr. Camirand's wife, the daughter of one of the foremen at the mine, the parish priest's housekeeper and a bevy of other women as well. Including Flore Obomsawin.

In those days, Flore was cleaning house for a number of people in Sioux Junction. She was a good worker, and her employers respected her because she had left the reserve, where she was born, and was fending for herself. They thought that she could easily have slipped into what they saw as the usual Indian pattern: get herself pregnant at fourteen, again at sixteen, go on welfare for the next twenty years, drink, sleep with anyone at all, anywhere at all. Or go to Toronto and become a hooker. In their eyes, Flore was a conscientious young girl of twenty who would make someone a good wife some day and raise happy, healthy children.

She wasn't so well liked at the reserve, where she was called Apple—red on the outside but white on the inside. Flore paid no attention to them: she wanted to make something of her life. Not for nothing, she would say, was she the descendant of Byron Miles and Charlemagne Ferron, Sioux Junction's cofounders. She had good blood in her veins, and she intended to let it show.

But the charms of Christos Sperdouklis, the handsome Figaro who had such a way with women, proved difficult to resist. Not that he was always making passes at women—it was just that, when women looked at him, they *wanted* him to make passes at them. And Flore, it must be said, was no babe in the woods. She had been sexually active since the age of thirteen—beginning with a thirty-

year-old mine worker who had brought her presents. After that she
had had a number of Sioux friends on the reserve. No one there paid
much attention to the niceties of romance, nor was the sensual
Indian in his natural state, as depicted in so many books written by
whites, anywhere in evidence. After three or four years, however,
she settled down. She wanted a different kind of life: she dreamed
of learning a trade, becoming a secretary or a hairdresser, travelling,
getting a job in Montreal or Toronto, meeting a man who would give
her security, children, a nice home. In the meantime, she decided,
she would clean houses in Sioux Junction; the pay wasn't bad, and
after a year or so she'd be able to get away.

Until then, she'd been incredibly lucky as far as men were
concerned. She had never practised any kind of contraception, but
had so far managed to stay out of trouble. She'd even begun to
wonder whether she was sterile. Two of her aunts had been unable
to bear children; why not her?

So when the handsome young Christos Sperdouklis made a
pass at her behind M. Grandmaître's harpsichord, which he'd been
repairing and she'd been dusting, the ambitious young Flore
Obomsawin seized her chance.

A month later, Figaro skipped town. He calmly announced
one day that he had finally saved up enough money to open a Greek
restaurant in Toronto. He knew that little Flore had completely lost
her head over him, but what could he do? He had been engaged
since birth to a sweet young virgin in Greece who was waiting to
board a ship for Canada the moment he sent for her. Sorry, honey
chile, but it's toot-toot-Tootsie, good-bye. And that goes for all the
others, too.

That was in April. In December, Flore gave birth to Thomas.
The arithmetic wasn't complicated: Figaro had flown the coop just
in time.

One morning she had just got up and vomited, and after that
she knew. Poor Flore, she said to herself, they always told me it

would happen this way, that this is what it was like to be pregnant. No need even to go to see Dr. Camirand. Christos had taken off three days earlier; he'd known, too.

Being pregnant and unmarried was no joke. There was no one she could confide in, no one she could talk babies to, although there were plenty of people who would step carefully around the topic, willing to talk animatedly about nothing at all rather than express an honest sympathy with her plight. Flore understood that, too.

Obviously there could be no question of going back to the reserve, where she would be ineligible for social assistance; no one on the reserve wanted her back, anyway. Everyone in her family was either dead or had moved off long ago. For a while, Flore didn't know what she was going to do.

Fortunately, not everyone in Sioux Junction was against her. There was M. Grandmaître, for example, who had been expecting trouble from the start and who even felt partly responsible for it, having been the one to bring Figaro into the picture in the first place. He paid her a visit, overcoming his own shyness, and asked her who the father was. She confirmed his suspicions; besides Obomsawin, he was the only other person who ever knew the truth, and she made him swear not to tell a soul. He gave her his word. As he was leaving, he turned to Flore—who had dissolved into tears—and said to her: "My child, if you ever need anything, anything at all, you let me know. Money, it doesn't matter what, don't be shy. I've got more than enough for myself. And when he grows up, bring him to me and I'll teach him everything I know. Even music, if that's what you want ..."

Omer Grandmaître was as good as his word. He often helped Flore get through the rough patches, and was as devastated as she was when the Mormons took Thomas away from her. When the boy returned home, Omer was one of the first people he went to see, and the old man broke down and wept for joy. Thomas had learned to draw while he was in the United States; Omer recognized his talent right away, encouraged him to develop it and even bought him his first brushes and paints. He also instilled in Thomas a love for poetry and music. Obom still talks about the great composers as if they were close personal friends of his, a habit he picked up from his old mentor. Omer would always be saying things like: "Chopin used to go out with a woman named George Sand, who wrote books; and Lizst was Wagner's father-in-law, did you know that? They were a very musical family. Johann Christian Bach, now, he was the eleventh son of Johann Sebastian, who was the best musician of the lot." Omer would recount all this while sucking on his pipe, resting between violin repairs. And even though it's true that Obomsawin never loved anyone in his life, he readily admits that his love for art was fostered by Omer Grandmaître.

There was also Dr. Camirand. He and his wife already had five children, but they offered to adopt Flore's baby all the same. No one need know, Mme Camirand told her, and he'll be just fine with us. Mme Camirand had her own ideas about who the child's father was, and she was very persistent. But Flore held her ground. The rest of the story we know.

No, it certainly was no joke to be pregnant and unmarried. Mme Richer, for example, who was one of the women Flore "did" for, told her straight off the bat that she had better look elsewhere for work from now on. "You understand my problem, Flore," she said. "I have my children to think about. I can't have them asking me questions about things I don't know the answers to myself. Just who is the baby's father, anyway?" Flore left the house without a word.

Christos Sperdouklis never returned to Sioux Junction. He opened the first Greek restaurant in Toronto, launching a craze that earned him tons of money, and then, his fortune made and his children all grown up, he returned to Greece to live out his last days. Before reaching Toronto, however, it seems he made his way through several other towns in northern Ontario, leaving a child in each of them. Rumour has it.

It sounds funny, but Thomas Obomsawin never displayed any interest in getting to know his father. One day, when he was practically grown up, Flore told him who his father was, but he never wished to see him or to know anything at all about him.

As Obom's third biographer, I knew Omer Grandmaître and his house full of music. It was Omer, in fact, who told me the story of Christos Sperdouklis, the Greek Figaro.

"He was an Adonis," Omer told me. "Strong, virile. If I had half his looks I wouldn't have been a bachelor all my life, I can tell you that. I knew he had an eye for the ladies, but what could I say? It was none of my business. But little Flore, now, there I felt I had to do something. I loved that child; she deserved better than to be stuck with an illegitimate baby at her age.

"I always knew Christos would make something of himself, you know. There was something special about him, something out of the ordinary. Oh, I'm not talking about his restaurants or his hundred thousand dollars a day or whatever he made from them; that doesn't interest me at all. Any lunkhead can work sixteen hours a day and get rich. No, what Christos did that made him special—listen, now, because this is important—the best thing Christos ever did in his life was to father Thomas Obomsawin. The painter. He was a dirty son of a bitch to Flore and I'll never forgive him for that. But he gave the world an artist."

And yes, it was thanks to Christos that Obom's full name is Thomas Christophe Obomsawin. Flore figured that Christos must be Greek for Christophe, you see. Thomas never used it, of course, it's only the English who call him Thomas C. Obomsawin. Because of that English biography of him, the first one, called *The Life and Paintings of Thomas C. Obomsawin: A Canadian Indian Painter*. That's why.

8

If the first two biographies of Obom were full of inaccuracies, exaggerations and other stupidities, it was Roland's fault.

Roland Provençal. He still lives in Sioux Junction. You can see him there any day of the week.

Poor Roland, if you believed everything he told you, if you laid all his supposed exploits out on the ground end to end, he'd have to be at least two hundred years old. Not that anyone ever calls him a liar to his face. He gets mad very easily if anyone ever questions anything he says. And I mean mad: he shouts insults at them, stomps out of the room, slams the door. But then he comes back the next day with the same story, as if nothing had happened. So people just let him ramble on. Poor Roland.

Of course, he believes that everything he says is God's own truth. I'm sure he believes every word of it.

For example, he'll be talking about all the places he's worked in his life. Now, Roland is sixty-six years old, but to hear him you'd swear he'd been working much longer than that.

"When I was a lad," he told me once, "I fought in a lot of wars. Europe, Africa, Asia. Three, all told. Not like soldiers today, who sit around on their backsides with nothing to do. I mean real wars! Three of the bastards. Against the Germans, the Chinese and the Ay-rabs. The first time I fought was with the English, then the Americans and then the French.

"The English aren't bad, at least they feed their troops real food. The Americans are well armed—they've got plenty of money—but as soldiers they aren't worth a pitcher of spit. As for the French, they're nothing but a bunch of fairies. No wonder they've lost every war they've been in.

"The ones I like to fight against best are the Germans. They're tough, but they're fair. After the fight's over they'll buy you a round of schnapps and a glass of beer. They know how to behave in a war. The Chinese aren't bad that way, but goddamn it they make poor soldiers. I knew a Chinaman in Toronto once, used to deliver Chinese food, he was the goddamned clumsiest son of a bitch I ever met in my life. You put a bunch of them in uniform and they'll end up shooting themselves and each other. If I was the Russian or the American government, I'd declare war on China tomorrow: it'd be over in two weeks, and the rest of the world could take it easy instead of worrying itself sick over nothing. And the Ay-rabs, don't talk to me about them. I'd take fifty Germans ahead of a million Ay-rabs any day. You *swear* at them and they fall down, for Christ's sake. Even the Jews are kicking the shit out of them. Have you ever heard of anything so ridiculous in all your life? Eh?

"No sir, there's nothing like a German when it comes to war. The French are a bunch of faggots. The French-*Canadians* aren't worth much either, but them others from France, forget it. I wouldn't fight with them again if you paid me. All right, maybe the Vandoos were a good unit once, but not any more, not today. They've got cat piss for blood, I'm telling you."

Roland didn't like English Canadians, either. He believed them to be a degenerate race. Ditto the Americans.

"Listen," he said. "Canadians are shit. Americans the same. I know, I worked on construction with the bastards for thirty years. Ten years in Canada, fifteen years in the States and twenty years in Russia. And in my humble opinion the Canadians and the Americans can't hold a candle to the Ruskies."

Then someone asked him how he came to be working for the Russians. "Where was that, Roland?"

"Whadya mean, where was that, Roland?" he said hotly. "Where the hell do you think it was? Where would *you* go to find Russians, eh? I worked twenty-five years for them, and I know them like the back of my hand. They pay good wages, they like people who work hard, they like good work, they pay on time, and they don't haggle over the price, either. If they like what you do, they pay up and Bob's your uncle. And there's the extras on top of that— which you would know if you'd spent as much time with them as I have—all the women you want, all the vodka 'n' orange juice you can drink. No sir, you can take my word for it, next to the Russians, the Canadians and Americans aren't worth a pinch of coon shit."

It was Roland Provençal who saw Obom setting fire to his mother's house. He was a witness for the prosecution at the trial. He lived across the street from the burnt house, in a unit owned by the Thunder Bay office of the Ministry of Community and Social Services, who bought it from the mining company for a dollar when the mines shut down. All kinds of people lived in these houses— mostly loony-tunes from the provincial mental hospital, released as outpatients because, at $2000 per day per bed, the ministry couldn't afford to keep them locked up any more. The provincial government in Toronto wanted to integrate the less dangerous among them into residential neighbourhoods, the schizophrenics, the manic-depressives, those who could feed themselves and remember to take their pills. A lot of them preferred to stay close to their former home on Queen Street West, in Toronto, but a number of them were moved into small towns in northern Ontario, where the cost of living wasn't so high. A few of these trickled into Sioux Junction, where the cost of living was pretty close to zero.

Roland was already living in the house when the mine closed. He rented a room in the basement. When the ex-patients from the loony bin began to arrive, he told them he was the manager of the building. No one questioned this statement, and after that whenever anyone asked him what he did for a living he'd say: "I'm a manager."

There was another tenant living in the house at that time. This was the Great Depression, whom the Constants had kicked out of the Logdrivers Hotel in order to make room for guests. Thus the Great Depression, who hardly ever spoke a word to anyone, found himself living in a house full of other crazy people who never stopped talking. There was one old Hungarian who spent his time writing letters to the prime minister: during the day, he did almost nothing but type. When he wasn't typing, he was complaining to the manager: "There's a woman in the house," he told Roland the other day, "who walks naked all night long. I reported her to the prime minister of Canada."

"Jesus Christ," Roland replied. "You crazies are driving me up the wall."

Another time, the same Hungarian confided in Roland: "I secretly married the Queen of England last March, in a church in Ottawa. On Elgin Street."

Roland was having trouble controlling his temper. "Will you kindly take your Queen of England and get out of my room, you crazy son of a bitch! I've had it up to here with your stories!"

Roland was discovering that being a manager was not always easy. At least the Great Depression was quiet, he muttered to himself, compared to all these idiots from Toronto.

9

Everything that can be said about Obomsawin's paintings has already been said. Or almost everything.

Obom's first biographers wrote a lot about his techniques and his successes. No point in repeating here their learned pronouncements upon his "graphic ellipticism," his "fragmented perspective," the "sonority of his coloration" and the "sociolinguistic significance of his symbolism." The two biographers were as alike as two peas in a pod, even though the first one wrote in English and the second in French. The recipe was the same for both books: take a full-page reproduction, add a page of text, two pages of bibliography, sprinkle in a few modest raptures, a pinch of exclamation points, a dollop of question marks, then dry thoroughly, allow to remain totally disconnected, and voilà. You'd think the two books were written by the same author. The first was called *The Life and Paintings of Thomas C. Obomsawin: A Canadian Indian Painter* and was written by Greta French, an art history professor at Ryerson Polytechnical Institute in Toronto. The title of the second was *Thomas Obomsawin:*

La nouvelle peinture amérindienne; its author, Denis Jalbert, was a Montreal doctor, art critic and a big collector of primitive art. Both books were self-published in small but elegant editions, and both were widely quoted in the press, in Canada as well as abroad: copies of them could be found in every major capital city and every university library in Canada.

Proof of the high quality of these studies may be found in the fact that whenever the Canadian government made a gift of an original Obomsawin canvas to some visiting head of state, the painting was accompanied by one of the two biographies in an authentic moose-hide binding. Former U.S. president Richard Nixon received a huge painting and the English biography; so did Golda Meir. French versions went to the prime minister of Zimbabwe and the first secretary of the Soviet Communist Party—who at the time was Brezhnev. Obom was never very impressed by that, by the fact that his paintings were chosen as gifts for foreign dignitaries. "Give 'em something like that," he said, "a painting or an Eskimo carving, what's the difference? It's just another 'photo opportunity,' makes Canada look good, lets 'em say, 'See how good we treat our Indians?' What am I supposed to do, stand up and cheer?"

Still, having his paintings chosen as official gifts didn't hurt Obom's career any. On the contrary. On each occasion the press release from the prime minister's office declared: "The Prime Minister presented to his prestigious guest a magnificent painting by the famous Canadian Amerindian graphic artist Thomas Obomsawin." These paintings can now be seen in Paris, London, Washington and Moscow. And it was gratifying to the citizens of Sioux Junction that these official communiqués also mentioned the birthplace of the famous painter: nice to see one of our own boys making good in the outside world.

Obom, though, made it a point never to attend any of these official presentation ceremonies. Which was too bad, because all of

Sioux Junction would have been able to see him on television.

Another thing Obom never did was read either of the books that had been written about him. He had had a few copies lying around, since they'd been sent to him free, but he gave most of them away to friends. He wasn't even remotely interested in them.

The books were well enough done, needless to say. The writers were serious people who had done much to advance Obom's career. For a painter, having a book written about you can mean the difference between obscurity and fame: it means you're not just another run-of-the-mill dauber. It helps sales, too. Still, Thomas had no desire even to meet the authors.

Obomsawin made no public statements concerning the biographies. Privately, though, he had lots to say about them:

"Do you like the books that were written about you, Obom?" I asked him once.

"No sir," he said. "No good."

"Why not?"

"I don't know those guys, and they don't know me. You'd think they would at least give me a call, eh? Just to say hello. But no, not even."

"Nonetheless, they did make you better known. They made you respectable."

"I don't give a shit about that. I don't need them to make me respectable."

And it was true that neither of the two biographies was without fault. Each one contained flagrant errors of fact. Worse than that, though: they both ... let's say ... embellished certain aspects of Obom's life. In certain cases, they went so far as to invent whole episodes.

But what Obomsawin had against them most was not that they invented certain facts, but that they left certain other facts out.

10

Everyone in Sioux Junction calls him the Great Depression.

He's not a bad fellow, not dangerous or anything. He's just depressed. Every day he walks through the village, staring at the sidewalk, dragging his feet. He isn't hard to recognize: he always wears jeans, a black sweatshirt and a Basque beret. If you meet his eyes he looks away. He never smiles and hardly ever speaks to anyone. Until recently, he lived at the Logdrivers Hotel, but the Constants kicked him out to make room for the two lawyers, so now he lives in Roland's house.

Roland shouldn't complain. The Great Depression's quiet, clean, pays his rent on time. But he always seems sad: just looking at him is enough to plunge anyone into a depression.

And he has a story, like most people. He's a social worker who came to Sioux Junction about four years ago, when the village was just beginning to shut down. There was a lot of unemployment here then, and all the social problems associated with that, so there was a lot of work for someone in his field.

When people got to know him, they realized he wasn't just another social worker. He was very well educated, for one thing: he had attended the Jesuit College in Sudbury, then the University of Montreal, then a university in England, then another one in the States. He had worked for two years in Africa and a year in Papua New Guinea, then taught at McGill and York. He was a cultivated man; he had seen a lot of the world and could talk interestingly about it. That is, when he talked.

And he had guts. He could have stayed on as a professor in Toronto or some other city, but he decided to come to Sioux Junction to work with real people who had real problems. He also wanted to conduct a study on Indians and on ghost towns in northern Ontario. He had written books in both official languages, which was something.

The depression hit him about two years after he got here. It should be mentioned that he lived alone. He had been married, but his wife hadn't wanted to follow him up north, preferring to stay behind in Toronto with their daughter. That probably hadn't helped.

When he first arrived in Sioux Junction—according to Roland, who occasionally hits on the truth—he talked about nothing but how the whites had mistreated the Indians, and went around saying that it was time to redress that wrong. He went out to the reserve often and visited the Indians in their rundown shacks, listening to their complaints. He believed everything they told him: the white man stole the land from the Indian, the white man raped Indian women, the white man wanted to keep everything for himself, the white man destroyed anything that came between him and a decent profit and, once that profit was made, the white man disappeared.

The social worker brought these stories back to Sioux Junction with him, saying they were all true and that something had to be done about them.

He was good with the Indians. He knew how to talk to them, even when they were drunk. He'd wake up in the morning and there'd be eight of them camped out in his living room, and his fridge would be empty before he had time to brush his teeth. One of the Indians even gave him a headband woven out of colourful cloth with the words "This man is a friend of the Indians" around it. He was so proud of it he wore it everywhere.

One day when he was coming back from the reserve he gave a lift to four Indians who were hitchhiking into town. There weren't a lot of cars on the road. Only the social worker knows what really happened, but it seems that the four Indians kicked the shit out him and stole his jeep. They beat him up so badly that he had to be airlifted out to the hospital in Thunder Bay. He was there for two months; when he got out, he returned to Sioux Junction. He had lost his headband during the fight, and never did get it back.

Ever since then he's been on sick leave from the Ontario Ministry of Community and Social Services. He watches the daily depletion of the village, but still says it's the fault of the whites. From time to time, he'll show you his scars from the time he was beaten and robbed, and he'll say that, too, is the fault of the whites. His brush with death hasn't changed his outlook one bit: whenever he meets an Indian now, he asks for forgiveness, his eyes filled with tears. He's a sad case.

But he seems to be getting better. He may even go back to work for the ministry, though probably in a different region. Meanwhile, he spends his days writing, going for frequent walks, looking depressed. He takes all his meals in his room—pork and beans, cans of spaghetti, gallons of tea. He eats a lot of chocolate bars and cookies. He's the Constants' best customer at their little grocery store behind the hotel. It's also said that he lies naked on his bed all night doing crossword puzzles. He says it polishes his French. According to Roland, anyway.

He has only one friend in the village—Obomsawin. Lately, the two have been spending all their time together.

One last observation: Roland may have forgotten, but it should be mentioned that the Great Depression was born in Sioux Junction, which may explain why he stays on here.

11

One of Obomsawin's huge murals depicts the splendour of Sioux Junction.

The mural was commissioned when Obom was just beginning to paint. The mine was in full swing and the Sauvé brothers' sawmill employed three hundred men. So much money was rolling into Sioux Junction that the municipal council suspended land taxes on certain kinds of property, and the school board was considering the construction of a high school. The historical paintings commissioned from the young local painter were like the icing on a huge cake.

I've already described the first mural, which showed the arrival of the two founders and their works. The later murals depict the fruition of these works.

Charlemagne Ferron and Byron Miles both became very rich very quickly. When prospectors discovered large deposits of gold and iron ore north of the town site, Miles lost no time buying up the mineral rights for all the land within a hundred-mile radius of Sioux

Junction. To raise the capital, he sold his forestry rights to his old friend Charlemagne Ferron, who was then the mayor of Sioux Junction and had already brought in large numbers of farmers from the Beauce region of Quebec to colonize the area. Charlemagne offered his farmers jobs in the forest to help them pay off their farms more quickly. At the same time, Miles continued to import workers from Wales, Ireland, Czechoslovakia and Rumania. Before long Sioux Junction had adopted quite a cosmopolitan air; there were fourteen languages spoken in the village. Under Charlemagne Ferron's intelligent leadership, Sioux Junction became the first officially bilingual village in Ontario: the proceedings of the municipal council and the two school boards, Catholic and Protestant, both of which were founded and presided over by Ferron, were conducted in English one week, and French the next.

All was going well. Except for the Sioux living just north of the Wicked Sarah, who gradually lost all their land and were shifted to a reserve even farther north. They managed to keep their ancestral hunting and fishing rights, but game was becoming increasingly difficult to find. This too was shown on Obomsawin's mural. It was said that Obomsawin's great-grandmother, the original Obomsawin—who had been given that name by Ferron and Miles—had gone to the Sioux reserve to die; she left her children in Sioux Junction and never saw them again. One of her sons had married an Irish woman, but the eldest, Francis, married a young girl from the Beauce. There were thus two Metis branches of the family, an English and a French side. The English Obomsawins left Sioux Junction around 1940, changing their name to Saween; the French Obomsawins stayed in Sioux Junction and kept their name intact.

Francis Obomsawin was never allowed to forget the fact that he was a half-breed. The sons-in-law of Charlemagne Ferron—the Sauvé brothers who owned the sawmill—were pleased enough to have Francis work for them, but they never invited him into their homes for fear of offending Charlemagne's wife. Charlemagne hadn't hidden from her the possibility of his being the father of Obomsawin's children, including Francis. (When prosperity reached Sioux Junction, Charlemagne had married the daughter of one of his farmers, a woman named Martha, who was as beautiful as a morning in spring, but as rigid as a ramrod in all matters religious and moral. Charlemagne had to re-embrace the Catholic Church before she would consent to marry him. The couple had only two children, both girls, now married to the Sauvé brothers from Montreal. If there was one word that could never be spoken in the Ferron household, it was "Obomsawin.")

As a bastard, Francis Obomsawin had plenty of work and enough to eat during his lifetime, but no more. He built a house in Sioux Junction, started a family, and maintained cordial—though not intimate—relations with Charlemagne, the man he believed to be his father. But when Ferron died, Martha had Obomsawin fired from the mill: she wanted nothing from her husband's former life to remind her of what she considered to be his all-too-heroic exploits. Without a word, Francis moved out to the reserve. His children, however, had developed a taste for town life, and one after another they moved into the city. Only one daughter, Flore, dared to return to Sioux Junction.

Knowing Ferron's unorthodox personality and his adventurous past, the townspeople were astonished at the coolness he exhibited towards Francis, but it must be said that when prosperity came to Sioux Junction, religion followed close behind. Martha agreed to marry Charlemagne—who at the time was forty years old—upon condition that they have a Catholic ceremony and that all their children be raised as Catholics. Charlemagne agreed without thinking much about it one way or another. Before long, priests began to move in, and then nuns and lay brothers to teach in the schools.

Until Ferron's death, religion had not played a major role in Sioux Junction. Like many enlightened seigneurs before him, Charlemagne had organized life in his village according to liberal, physiocratic and essentially secular principles. He encouraged material prosperity, an appreciation of the value of property, work and education, and official bilingualism. He opened Sioux Junction's first school at his own expense, and lectured there himself from time to time, dropping in to take over this or that class as the mood struck him. Before a respectful but somewhat nervous teacher, he would talk to the students about all the new ideas floating about in his head: how Man was descended from the apes, for example, or that there was no Hell, and that Science had unravelled all the mysteries of the universe, and that it was Man's sacred right to overthrow bad governments. Ferron's physiocratic leanings were felt most strongly at the municipal council, however: there, following some arcane principle known only to himself, he would have deciduous trees planted along all the east/west streets in the town and conifers along all the north/south streets. And he undertook the naming of all streets as his own special province—Voltaire Avenue; Garibaldi Road; Locke Lane; Montesquieu, Papineau and Chénier streets, among others. And he invited the celebrated Médéric Dutrisac to set up an experimental farm in Sioux Junction, where he could conduct his experiments in animal mutagenics—crossing moose and deer, cats and rabbits, buffaloes and Holsteins—for the purpose of relieving hunger in the world.

As Sioux Junction's founding mayor and the riding's first elected Member of Parliament, Ferron was able to ensure that the railroad passed through his town—and he reaped enormous profits from a little judicious buying and selling of land along the way. He was also careful to build up the fortunes of his two sons-in-law, who were good workers and quick learners. Through all this, Ferron remained proudly liberal-minded, welcoming Catholic clergymen who came to teach the town's children but at the same time holding himself quite apart from religious matters. His former apostasy faded into nothing more than an amusing memory, something to be brought out every now and then and gazed at with a kind of private pride.

He was a great man, filled with ideas of progress and reason. It was through his efforts that Sioux Junction was favoured with a telegraph office, radio reception, a bilingual newspaper (which he owned), a doctor (who visited once every two months), a small hospital, a telephone switchboard, the first hotel with a liquor licence (which he also owned), and, finally, a genuine Austrian pastry chef—a former prisoner of war from a camp near Kapuskasing—who opened a real Konditorei in which patrons could eat Kaiser cream puffs while listening to Strauss on the gramophone.

Indirectly, he was also responsible for bringing in the priests. It was really through his wife, who wanted to convert her husband to the true faith, but it was also partly his own doing: he wanted cheap teachers for his school. Throughout his life, however, he never gave in to the pressures exerted on him by the clergy, even though it must be said that the interests of Sioux Junction weren't so badly served by them after all.

So Ferron died. Practically before he was cold in his grave the Sauvé brothers ordered their employees to attend Mass every Sunday on pain of dismissal. All lapsed Catholics and alcoholics were fired, and the brothers took it upon themselves to hold back a tithe from their lumberjacks' wages for the Church. Other things changed as well. Agriculture died, for one thing, and the Beaucean farmers' sons were forced to go to work for the Sauvés, who had a free hand in the town. No more factory workers' association, no more company picnics, no more alcohol in the lumber camps—one whiff and you were out on your ear! Old Madame Ferron, Charlemagne's widow, was entirely devoted to the works of the clergy in Sioux Junction, and her sons-in-law were entirely devoted to her. They had to be; otherwise, she might cut them out of her will and leave her fortune to the Church.

The priests had to conduct an extra four Masses every Sunday, there were so many people coming to church. Five of the six hotels in town had to close down—the one exception was the Logdrivers, which at that time belonged to the Sauvés. The library, opened by Charlemagne, was closed by his heirs; soon the newspaper followed suit. Street names were changed, too: Voltaire Avenue became Notre-Dame Street, Montesquieu became Boulevard of the Precious Blood, Garibaldi Road became Calvary Crescent. Indian children attending the French school in town were shipped back out to the reserve, where the federal government had just opened an English school. Two new churches were built. Médéric Dutrisac was denounced as an atheist and a communist and run out of town, along with his unholy circus of fabulous beasts: his long-eared cats, his humpless buffaloes, his wolf-dogs. The French Canadian people of Sioux Junction had returned to the fold.

This fit of religious fervour gripped the whole town. In the old days, the French, Rumanian and Czech miners had been on good terms with the French-Canadians who worked in the lumber camps. After the death of Charlemagne, however, relations became strained. Take the case of Bergman, for example, the only Jew in Sioux Junction. He was forced to leave town when the priests discouraged their parishioners from buying from him, saying his ancestors had crucified Christ. Eventually, the village split into two clans, anglophone and francophone, with the river running between them. The two sides never mixed; Sioux Junction West spoke English, Sioux Junction East spoke French. The English worked the mines, the French worked in the woods. In the town council, the English representatives conducted their affairs amongst themselves and rarely included the French representatives, who anyway lost interest in public office after the death of Ferron. Slowly, the rupture crystallized into a permanent rift. Sioux Junction wasn't a pleasant place to live any more. The Austrian baker, disgusted with the whole sad business, moved on.

Another indirect victim of Charlemagne's death was Byron Miles. The two men had remained friends throughout their lives, both knowing that they would agree on everything that concerned the well-being of the town. With the enormous wealth he derived from the mine, Miles racked up an impressive array of good works on his side. But Ferron's death provoked in Miles, who had never in his life thought of anything except making money, a sort of crisis of reflection. His wife, Rhian, had died a few days before Ferron, and Miles gave all his property to his children, who lost no time selling off the mineral rights to a large multinational and moving away with their newfound wealth. One of them, Julian Miles, who had studied overseas, accepted a Chair in Philosophy at Oxford, where he led the idle life of an intellectual with a private income for the rest of his days. Another—a daughter—married a penniless German baron while on vacation in Italy. The others lived in New York and Boston. All of them are dead now, and left no descendants.

Abandoned like King Lear, Byron Miles renounced his Anglican faith and resurrected his original name: Balthazar Szepticky. He relearned Ukrainian from the few retired miners who still spoke it, and had a Ukrainian church built in town complete with an onion-topped roof. He appointed himself sexton, and spent the remainder of his days praying and carving church benches out of solid oak. One morning, in August, he was found dead on one of the last of his woodworking projects.

You can still see that bench. Obomsawin made it a public monument by dragging it from the church and setting it on Main Street, where he sits every day with his back turned to the Wicked Sarah.

Obomsawin was never paid a cent for his historical paintings or his murals. The commission had been approved by the municipal council back when Sioux Junction was one of the most prosperous communities in northern Ontario. Everyone owned a television; the sons and daughters of the rich went away to the city to go to school; there was a theatre, two cinemas, a cultural centre and new cars in every garage. The women took classes in gourmet cooking from a master chef who came up from Toronto once a month; the doctor and the lawyer took long vacations in Europe, the Sauvé brothers went to Bermuda every winter, and the American owners of the mine came up every fall to hunt bear and moose, and lived in huge, luxurious, private cottages built and maintained especially for them.

Then, one day, the mine began to lay off workers. At about the same time, the Sauvé brothers decided to diversify their holdings by investing in high-return enterprises in southern Ontario—for their children, they said. They wanted to provide a cushion against the day when there were no more trees in the North. There would always be time to sell later to a competitor who was less under the gun. For Sioux Junction, though, it meant fewer jobs, fewer workers, less money and less culture. The municipal council even had to reinstate property taxes. In order to avoid paying Obom for his paintings, the councillors pretended to find them immoral and historically inaccurate.

Curiously, Obomsawin didn't complain about this breach of contract. He seemed happy enough to be reimbursed for his expenses and to receive a small forfeiture fee. He kept the paintings, of course; or rather, he gave them to his mother, who said she needed something to liven up her walls. He could have railed against the council for making him work eighteen months for nothing, but as he told me later, he was glad enough to hang on to the paintings. He hated them. No one can paint pure History, he said; it's always the artist and the artist's own time that is represented. You can't escape it: look at the Crucifixion scenes painted in the Middle Ages, which depict Mary wearing mediaeval clothing and the Roman soldiers in chain mail carrying British crossbows, and the Pharisees dressed like Flemish bürgermeisters.

Obomsawin's historical paintings, then, were a kind of apprenticeship. The portraits of nuns and aldermen that he did at this time were mostly opportunities for him to observe, to select, to decide what it was he really wanted to depict. He learned that the canvas of History is always tainted by half-lies, and that truth in Art can only be coaxed out in fragments.

12

Obomsawin's trial followed its normal course.

Obviously it was no longer the same trial it had been at the beginning. It had become something of a cause célèbre. The sessions themselves hadn't changed, but since the trial began Sioux Junction had become a different place entirely. It was sad, but it was true.

First there was the Logdrivers Hotel: in less than four weeks it had undergone a complete change of face. From now on the three rooms were taken by the judge—who had the biggest—the Crown prosecutor and the lawyer for the defence. The former tenant had been tossed out into the street. The twelve jurors already lived in town, so they didn't need rooms anyway.

But there were others. Witnesses never seemed to stop turning up. Character witnesses for the defence, hostile witnesses for the prosecution, and all of them seemed to come from out of town. Psychiatrists from Toronto—one of whom said Obomsawin was in a short-term depression, another that he found him to be a manic-depressive—and art dealers, insurance agents, experts in arson, legal advisors. They all came in by float plane, hung around for a day or two, left again, came back later. The hotel didn't have room for everyone at once, but Jo Constant was kept busy taxiing them back and forth between Lake Winnissogan and Sioux Junction, and for a small consideration he would find them temporary lodgings somewhere else in town.

Businesswise, things had never gone better for the Constants. They were going so well, in fact, that Mme Constant—Fat Cécile—no longer worked in the kitchen or did any other kind of household chore; she greeted the guests as they arrived in the lobby, wearing her black dress or her sea-blue suit with the white collar. She said it lent some dignity to the occasion. She felt she was living in a dream: she had people working for her; she was the *patronne*. She had gone out and hired one of the retired cooks from the lumber camp, and he was working strictly under her supervision. She had also brought in a few summer students from Thunder Bay to do the rooms and wait on the tables. She kept the books and managed the hotel's business while Jo drove his taxi and ran her errands. And every night, the two of them would saunter from table to table in the dining room, asking if everything was all right. Just like in real hotels.

And more and more often these days, the answer was yes. No more complaints about always eating the same thing, at any rate. In the old days there had been bacon and eggs for breakfast, ham sandwiches and cream of tomato soup for lunch, and caribou steak with boiled potatoes for dinner—day in, day out. No more. Cécile had sent Jo to the wholesaler's in Thunder Bay, and now he went every week. Meals had picked up considerably: vegetables from only slightly dented tins, fruit that was barely past its prime, sliced white bread, real meat—pork roasts, hips of beef—because guests had begun to tire of game, especially the long-term ones. Luckily, old Martin, the new cook, knew how to make plenty of things: pies, baked bean and rabbit casseroles, real Italian spaghetti. And there was no more bootleg wine or bathtub whiskey, either. Cécile had got in a few cases of beer and several gallons of good Canadian wine. There was even some cheap Niagara rosé to go with dessert from time to time, though that cost extra. Yes sir, it was a real hotel, with a real menu, daily specials and your choice of Jell-O or rice pudding.

Things turned up on the menu at the Logdrivers that no one in Sioux Junction had ever heard of before. Once Jo came back from Thunder Bay with a crate of kiwis. Kiwis. No one knew what they were. When Fat Cécile opened the box she called Jo over: "Hey smart-ass! What the hell are these things?"

"They're called kiwis."

"What are we supposed to do with them? They look like monkey balls."

"You eat them. They're good. Look." And he took a knife and cut one in half. Cécile wasn't impressed.

"They're still green."

"They're supposed to be green. Go ahead, try one. They're good."

He peeled the kiwi for her and she tasted it.

"You're right, for once, they do taste good. Go tell Martin to make something with them for dinner."

And from that day on there were kiwis in the Logdrivers' dining room—kiwi pies, kiwi tarts, kiwi pudding, kiwis and cream. The guests began to complain again.

Jo wasn't all that happy about the way things were going. He was working harder now than he had before his retirement. He'd gotten used to doing nothing except dream about having a full hotel; now that he had one, he was on the go from morning to night. And his wife was no more amiable than she'd been before. True, she no longer yelled at him in public, but in private she was worse than ever. She said mean things to him: he was a useless wimp; why couldn't he keep out of her way; he wasn't worth the trouble he caused. Poor Jo. In front of guests she was always after him to act more dignified, stand up straight, be polite. Like her. She forbade him to tell his favourite stories. She told him not to burp or fart at the table. She made him behave as though he were a real hotelier, and the Logdrivers were a real hotel.

"I don't want to hear about it, Jo Constant. Get this straight: it was you who dragged me here, so it's you who has to do what I tell you to do. Capiche?"

Jo couldn't wait for the trial to end. He wanted everything to go back to the way it was, when there were no paying customers, when the two of them had had some time to themselves. Nothing owed to anyone, no errands to run, get up when you feel like it. He couldn't help complaining to his wife.

"You just shut your big yap and get back to work, you measly little twerp! You wouldn't know your ass from a teakettle. Don't you understand what's happening here? Eh? Number one, this stupid hotel of yours hasn't made so much money since the day that Syrian bastard dumped it on you. Number two, suppose that stupid Indian bastard's trial goes on for another month. Number three, then suppose some other stupid bastard like you comes along and sees what a red-hot property this place is. If he's even half as stupid as you, he'll buy it, and we can laugh ourselves all the way to the bank. Give me five minutes to pack and it's see you in Florida, sucker!

"Now, did you get all that, Jo? No, I'll bet I lost you somewhere. Never mind. Listen, there's something else. I don't like it when you call me Cécile in front of the guests. It's demeaning. And it sets a bad example to the other staff, too. It's not professional. It isn't dignified. From now on, I want you to call me Mme Constant. Say, I'll have to ask Mme Constant. Or, I'll mention it to the proprietor. You know, as if you just work here. I think it'll make a better impression ...."

Jo looked down at his shoes. Maybe old Tub-of-Lard was right.

But goddamn it, he thought, things were a whole lot better around here in the old days, and I don't care who says they weren't. Son of a bitch, Obom, why'd you have to go set fire to your mother's house anyway?

Today there was good news: the judge had decided to prolong the trial for the rest of the summer. It was an unusual decision for the Supreme Court of Ontario, and Judge Kendrick had to make a special representation in Toronto, and arrange to take his summer vacation in the fall. The two lawyers didn't mind, though—quite the contrary. So things were looking up for the tourism business in Sioux Junction. Fat Cécile was so happy she decided to hold a party for the judge as a token of her appreciation. She'd found out it was his birthday, which made it all the better. "Poor man, he won't be able to celebrate with his family. We'll make him feel at home."

For his part, the judge was happy to spend a few more months in Sioux Junction. It might be a backwoods hole, but it was better than going home to Toronto. For one thing, his son had leukemia, and was getting worse, and the poor judge hated to watch his son suffer so much. For another, his wife was suing him for divorce on grounds of infidelity. And his daughter hadn't returned from her latest trip to Mexico, where she'd already been arrested once for drug trafficking. And his mistress was phoning him every day to ask him when he was going to wrap things up here and come back to live with her. Didn't he love her any more, et cetera, et cetera. If he was going to hear about problems, he'd just as soon hear about Obomsawin's problems. They were more interesting than his own, anyway. So he slowed down the proceedings. He wanted to hear from anyone who had three words to say about this great painter they were trying. It was his duty.

It was also the duty of the defence counsel, Jack Fairfield, who had lost every client he'd had because he drank like a fish, and who hoped to make a name for himself again by getting this Obomsawin character off the hook. The painter was becoming more famous every day. Details of the trial were turning up in the newspapers and even on television. Win a case like this and the clients would line up down the hall. No more worrying about his reputation then. He could even up his fees.

The Crown prosecutor was also happy. He had one ambition in life: to be made a judge as quickly as possible. He wanted the prestige, the increase in salary, the decrease in work, the ability to send his children to good schools. He also wanted to please his parents and impress his former classmates in law school, who had always treated him like an idiot. Fate had handed him a trial that was being talked about. Just yesterday, in the House of Commons, Liberal member Sheila Copps had posed some pretty penetrating questions about the case to the government. The prosecutor's name had been mentioned; that was good, his work was being noticed. Fate had also placed him in the eye of Judge Kendrick, who exerted considerable influence in the Ontario magistrature. A recommendation from him would go far. The Crown prosecutor intended to ask the judge for his support, so it was important that he make a good showing at this trial. And Sioux Junction wasn't such a bad place, when it came right down to it; his family probably wouldn't mind spending their vacation up here, and it would be one hell of a lot cheaper than a cottage on Georgian Bay. In short, the situation suited him to a T.

Mme Constant's idea of throwing a party, then, was a big hit. No one had any objections. Diversions were few and far between in Sioux Junction. She invited the whole town, which by now meant quite a few people. Most of the company houses the mine had built to provide cheap accommodation for its workers were filled up again, mainly by squatters who had come from God knows where, attracted by the flurry of activity surrounding the trial. They wouldn't be around for long. The mining company had sent people up to Sioux Junction to look into making the houses available for the use of witnesses and court officials connected with Obomsawin's trial, "as a gesture of good will." In fact, the mining company was hoping to reenter the Canadian business community, and wanted to defuse any ill will it had incurred by the sudden shutdown of the mine five years before. The trial provided a perfect opportunity for some good publicity; there were even rumours afloat that the mine might be reopened. It had been these rumours that had attracted the squatters, who turned up anywhere there might be work.

So there were a lot of people interested in Obomsawin's case. It may not have been the trial of the century for Canada, but it certainly was for Sioux Junction. Among the crowd flowing through the courtroom were numerous art dealers, who had come to see how much they could get for paintings by the man they now referred to as the Master. There were quite a few journalists, too, people with tape recorders, flash cameras, portapaks and microphones.

Most prominent among the latter was the famous Sigourney Wakefield, whose real name was Marcia Horowitz and who wrote a regular column in a Toronto daily called "Dear Ziggy," in which she answered hundreds of questions of such monumental import as: "I love my fiancé dearly. He is a very hard-working and sensitive man. But he has one serious flaw: he smells. How can I tell him without offending him?" Or, "I am getting married next month to the most beautiful girl in the world. She wants to wear a white gown, but I happen to know she is not a virgin. This seems dishonest to me, but she is adamant. How can I talk her out of it without implying that she is a slut? Please help!" And Dear Ziggy replies ....

Dear Ziggy and Obomsawin had been lovers at one time, back when Obom was in his early twenties and just beginning to make a name for himself. In fact, as she told a television interviewer, "I sort of made him famous. He left me, but I still care for him. I am here to support him morally. He is a great artist, no doubt, and he doesn't deserve all this. I am going to hire the best lawyers in Toronto to help him out." She said this on national TV, standing in front of the Logdrivers Hotel. The town felt honoured to have her here.

Yes sir, Sigourney Wakefield, still a beautiful woman, right here in Sioux Junction with a dozen of the most famous tabloid journalists in the country trailing behind her. The trial was even being reported in the United States. Obom was at the peak of his fame. Every rag in America was dying to get its hands on the novel Ziggy was writing about her love affair with the Master—but that was a secret. Don't tell a soul!

Needless to say, she wasn't staying at the Logdrivers—it was far too small for her and her entourage. She was in town for only an hour or two at a time anyway. Her hydroplane—lent to her by a wealthy Hamilton businessman—was kept at the ready on Lake Winnissogan. She would visit Obomsawin on his bench, talk to him for a few minutes, have her photograph taken with him, grant an interview or two to the reporters who had come up with her, then— fly the coop. Her plane would take off, with Ziggy, her two Pekingese and her bevy of reporters comfortably in it.

Mme Constant occupied herself with preparations for the party. Maybe Ziggy would be there. Wouldn't that be something! She'd probably bring her journalist friends with her. She might even mention the hotel and the Constants on television! Wouldn't *that* be something!

13

It's a small world.

And it's no bigger in Sioux Junction than anywhere else.

Ask Obom. He has travelled around the world and met people he knows in the damndest places. Japan, for example. He lived there for a year once, when he was working on a theory about the similarities between early Japanese prints and the figurative drawings of the Haida Indians in British Columbia. One day he was walking down a street in Kyoto and who should he run into but a brother—now defrocked—who had taught him mathematics at the reform school in Alfred, Ontario, and who was in Japan on a honeymoon with his new wife, a former nun whom Obomsawin also knew: she had been the vestry nun at Sacré-Coeur Jésus in Alfred. They recognized Thomas and asked him what he was doing in Japan, and they all chatted for a while. The ex-brother told Obom that he was proud of his former student, and that he should keep on painting. Then the two newlyweds walked off down the street. It's a small world.

Another time, Thomas met one of the Sauvé brothers on the slopes of Machu Picchu, in Peru. Bruno—the youngest member of the family that owned half of Sioux Junction—was in Peru with a woman who was not his wife. He was a bit embarrassed to find Thomas hiking along the same trail, but it was a narrow trail and there was no place to hide.

"Hey, Bruno!"

"Thomas? What the hell are you doing here?"

"Hiking. What are you doing here?"

"Me? Oh, I—I'm travelling around the world. For my health. Doctor's orders—he said I needed the rest. I decided to start in South America. I've never been here before. Er, have you met Gisèle? We're, er, travelling together. Gisèle, this is Thomas Obomsawin. He's an artist. He, er, makes paintings."

"Enchanté, Gisèle."

"Gisèle is a cousin of mine. From Montreal. I'm, er, paying her way, eh? She really needed a vacation because she just lost her husband. A few months ago. So listen, give me a call sometime, eh? I've got to run now, but, er, keep in touch."

And the two of them hurried off down the trail. It is a small world.

Another time it was Berlin. This was a long time ago—Obom's first trip to Europe. He didn't have a cent, of course. He'd just got out of prison and had decided to "lose himself," as he said, to give himself some fresh ideas. He had hitchhiked from Toronto to Montreal, and then from Montreal to the Gaspé. From there he had taken a fishing boat to Newfoundland, hopped a Portuguese freighter to Iceland, made it over to Denmark and then thumbed his way down through Europe, working here and there, sleeping wherever he could. To make some extra money for himself he drew portraits of tourists in parks and town squares. All in all he stayed overseas for two years. Without a passport. He knew he had to be careful, and he was. What good is a passport? he told himself. I'm an Indian. I don't even have a country. How can I have a passport if I don't have a country?

His two-year "Grand Tour" gave his other biographers the idea that he had gone to Europe to study painting. One of them even said he spent his formative years in Berlin. What a joke. The only truth in it was that he did spend more time in Berlin than anywhere else. But it wasn't by choice.

It was because of a woman. He wasn't in love with her—we've already established that he had never been "in love" with anyone. To this day no one can understand how he had managed to stay so long in Europe without a passport, and history cannot enlighten us on this point. However he had done it, he had managed to hang in until the Sunday he met Wiebke Haas. She taught Latin and French at the gymnasium in Berlin, though she was originally from the highlands of Sudetenland when it had still been part of Czechoslovakia. Obom had gone into a flea market to buy a sweater because winter was coming on, and Wiebke, who happened to be in the same place at the same time, had ended up acting as his interpreter. They left together, and stopped under a chestnut tree somewhere for a chat. She was a very beautiful woman, slightly taller than Obom, recently divorced—hardly in her thirties—with auburn hair. Obom offered to do her portrait for nothing. He didn't want her to go. He hadn't spoken French since leaving the Gaspésie. For once in his life, he felt the need to talk to someone. She didn't understand his French very well, and asked him in somewhat halting English where he was from. Canada? No kidding! She had a sister who had emigrated to Canada! What a small world! *Eine kleine Welt* ....

She had to run to a class, though, no time to sit for a portrait, but could he help her carry a heavy piece of furniture up to her flat? She had just bought it in the next street. On certain days of the month in Berlin people who wanted to get rid of articles of old furniture brought it to various designated streets and sold it instead of throwing it out; other people bought it, dragged it home, fixed it up and used it to furnish their apartments. Obom helped her carry a dresser up to her flat, and stayed for two months.

There were some good times, when he thought back on those days. They made love every night on an old leather sofa also rescued from the street sale. Wiebke loved him to distraction—or rather like someone who had been alone for a long time, which amounts to the same thing. She took him everywhere, introducing him to everyone she knew as her alingual Amerindian painter. As for Obom, he ate three meals a day, drank as much as he wanted and slept every night with a woman at the top of her form. He didn't exactly love her, perhaps, but she was very good to him. She had one strange habit, though: when they were making love, instead of turning the lamp off she liked to put a piece of old silk over the shade so she could see what they were doing. One night, when the piece of silk was in the laundry and she was in a particular hurry, she grabbed the first thing that came to hand and put it over the lamp. It was Obom's sweater, the one he had bought at the flea market the day they met. During the night the sweater must have sunk down and rested on the bulb, for in the morning Obom found a large, black hole in the middle of the back. Not being proud, he simply shrugged and put it on anyway.

No doubt it was this gaping love-wound in his back that drew the attention of the police, who arrested him that same day while he was pissing against the Berlin Wall—on the east side of the wall, where of course he had no business being in the first place. The East German police were doubly suspicious when they found he had no passport: no police force in the world likes foreigners without passports, especially foreigners without passports who dress like rubbies. Some of them can take it very seriously. Obom spent the next four months living on stale bread and water in a municipal holding tank, making rude drawings on the walls, before he finally managed to convince his interrogators that the language he was speaking was Canadian Metis. They had to send to Moscow for a specialist in Amerindian languages: they didn't know whether they were dealing with a CIA spy or a babbling idiot who wandered around without a passport talking in tongues.

Luckily for Obom, the Soviet specialist understood Sioux, and in his report he confirmed that Obom was who he said he was. So far so good. But what about the passport? During the four months of his incarceration, Wiebke had been hounding the Canadian consulate as well as the West German authorities. What in the name of heaven had Obomsawin been doing in East Germany? As it turned out, he had fallen in with a group of tourists from India, managing to fool the border guards with his dark skin. He said he wanted to see for himself if people living under a communist regime were as unhappy as everyone in the West said they were.

At last, to make a long story short, because of various pressures exerted by Ottawa, who wanted their Native Person returned, and thanks to the East German government, which didn't want to appear foolish and which had anyway decided that Obom was neither a CIA spy nor a famous Amerindian artist defecting to the East, Obom was deported. They brought him to Checkpoint Charlie, handcuffs chafing his wrists beneath the sleeves of his ragged sweater. After being locked up for four months, he was glad to be outside. And you'll never guess who was waiting for him on the western side, accompanied by a phalanx of American soldiers who stood with their rifles aimed at the squad of Russian soldiers who were also armed to the teeth: none other than Pierre Carrière, from Sioux Junction.

"Pete! What the hell are *you* doing here?"

"I came to get you, Thomas. You are being released and sent back to Canada."

"But why you?"

"I'm the Canadian consul at Stuttgart. They put me in charge of your case. I had to make all the arrangements, it was a real pain in the ass, but I didn't mind when I found out it was you. But don't tell anyone we come from the same village, they might find it suspicious. Come on, let's go."

"Jesus Christ, it's a small world. Don't you find, Pete?"

"Yes, you're right. But we have to hurry."

Peering through the early morning mist, Obom tried to find Wiebke. She wasn't there. There were, however, more policemen, this time West German, who immediately rearrested Obom and put him on the first plane for Canada. Pierre Carrière went with him to the British military airport as part of his official duty. In the car on the way they exchanged news. Stuttgart was Pierre's first posting since joining the Canadian diplomatic service.

"So what's it like, being a diplomat?"

"Obom, you are being deported. You can't go sauntering around foreign countries without a passport. If you want, I can get one for you, but you should count yourself lucky we were able to intervene on your behalf. You could have disappeared, Obom. Do you realize that? If it hadn't been for your friend, Mrs. Haas, we wouldn't even have known you were missing."

"Wiebke? That reminds me: listen, Pete, I won't get a chance to call her to thank her, my plane's leaving right away. Would you call her for me? You must know a few words of German. Will you call her?"

"Yes, all right, I'll do that."

Pierre still remembers Obomsawin, dressed like a tramp and

thin as a rail, but in a good mood, happy to be going home even if it was in a pair of handcuffs, making weak jokes.

"I thought people in the West were supposed to be freer than people in the East. They seem to get their handcuffs from the same place, at any rate."

Pierre Carrière never did call Wiebke. He didn't have her number and he felt he had already done enough for Obom. And he still had to make out a report on the whole affair. He didn't do too badly, though: for having effected the release of a Canadian citizen, he was promoted and given a post in the office of the minister of foreign affairs in Ottawa. When he returned to Canada, he got married, and not to just anyone, either. A man in his position needs a woman who knows how to conduct herself in public, who knows how to converse, how to be a good hostess.

Yes, things went well for Pierre. He married a young girl from a wealthy family who had studied English literature at university and had even come from Sioux Junction. Like Pierre, however, she knew enough not to mention it. Her name was Carmen Richer. Small world, isn't it?

14

Obomsawin earned a lot of money in his time.

It's the least known part of his life.

As far as Obom was concerned, everyone wanted to believe in the friendly, famous but starving artist. Not even his biographers mention the paintings that allowed him to live the life of Riley for nearly ten years—whiskey and cocaine galore, super jets whisking him around the world.

The paintings by Obomsawin hanging in the Hermitage Museum in Moscow and in the Beaubourg in Paris are not the ones that paid for his expensive habits. They're the ones he worked on the longest, and they're the ones no private collector could afford to buy. Government purchasers preferred them, and they are unquestionably his best work. But they are not the works that made him rich. His first biographers passed over these other paintings in silence, probably because they knew nothing about them.

I'd pass over them myself if I could, but Obom insisted. Tell the whole story or keep your mouth shut, he said. Come on, man, *sipwehtetan*!

At a certain point in his career, Obomsawin decided he'd had enough of starving to death. One day a painter from Ottawa, an amateur with more money than talent, said to him: "I know you, Obomsawin. You do good work. I've bought a couple of your paintings myself, and I've always thought you had talent. But surely you know that making art and making money are two different things. Here, let me show you."

Obom was interested. At the time, he didn't have a penny to his name. He wasn't selling and he hadn't done any useful work for three years. The Canadian government had bought a few canvases and placed them in foreign museums, but that had hardly been enough to keep him rolling in dough. And having a couple of books written about him didn't improve his situation either. He wanted a change. He wanted to make some fast money so he could take a long vacation and forget about his problems once and for all. To live high off the hog, for once in his life. So he went with the Ottawa man to the house of a third painter, a guy named Boivin.

Boivin wasn't a bad painter. But he drank like a fish and was always three sheets to the wind when he painted: he worked with a brush in one hand and a bottle in the other. "You know, Obom," he would say, "way down deep, I don't think I have complete confidence in my own talent. I just can't paint sober; I need stimulation. That's why I drink. Anyway, with a name like Boivin, what else can I do? I've got to live up to it, eh? Here, have a snort."

"Look at him, Obom," said the man from Ottawa. "He is one of the most gifted painters of his generation. He could do anything he likes. But he would be dying of starvation if it weren't for me. When I met him, his wife and children ate one meal every two days. Thanks to me, those days are over. 'Pull yourself together, man,' I said to him. 'You've got to earn a living. Do something simple that pays big bucks. Later, when you've made your nest egg, you can paint whatever the hell you want.'"

Obom was curious. He took a look at Boivin's work: it was all landscapes of the Ottawa area—the Rideau Canal, the Parliament Buildings, the Museum of Man, Byward Market. There were thousands of them in the house, those inoffensive little pastiches for tourists that turn up in the streets of Old Montreal and on rue du Trésor in Quebec City. No doubt about it, these postcard paintings paid well. And when he was done with them, Boivin had plenty of time to work on his more experimental stuff, his abstracts, the things he did for love. Obom asked to see some of them.

"My experimental stuff? Well, I haven't done any yet, actually. I'm waiting until I get a bit more money put away. At first I thought I could do both at the same time, but damn, it wasn't easy. But I'll get around to it sooner or later."

"How long has it been since you did any real work?"

"I don't know," Boivin shrugged. "Five, six years. It doesn't matter. It's like riding a bike, eh? You never forget how. I hope."

Obom was hooked. He decided to do the same thing. Money first, art second. The first painter—whose name was Langevin, by the way—was as pleased as punch to rope in the great Obomsawin.

"Look here, Obom," he said. "You come from northern Ontario, right? You must be able to paint a pretty good northern landscape. You know, one of those autumn scenes, the log cabin in the foreground, smoke rising out of the chimney. Or animal tracks in snow, that kind of thing. Winterscapes. Or how about a little stream with ice floating down it in spring? Can you do that? I tell you, man, paint a few of those and the world will beat a path to your door. They'll buy it by the shovelful, no kidding. And for a painter like you, there's nothing to it!"

Obom didn't need to be told twice. He set out at once to produce scenes from northern Ontario. He painted like a maniac. In one year he did six hundred of them—almost two a day! And he was staying with Langevin rent-free!

"You can pay me back when you make your first million," Langevin said. "Meanwhile, you've got to sell these. And there's no better salesman than the painter himself. I'll show you how it's done."

So Obomsawin learned how to sell. He teamed up with Langevin, and the two of them launched a series of "Creative Pictorial Workshops": Langevin delivered the public lectures and Obom did the demonstrations. It was like fishing in a barrel. Langevin told them that everyone had an artist locked up inside themselves, dying to get out, and that that artist was released as soon as they held a paintbrush and a palette in their hands. They only had to free themselves of their inhibitions.

"Let's say you want to paint a landscape," he told them. "Everyone likes a nice landscape. And there's nothing to it! All you need is some canvas, a few brushes, your favourite colours, and go to it! Let yourself go. Never mind how much talent you think someone else has—think about your own!

"Okay, we'll make a landscape. First you draw a line, like this. See how easy it is? Okay, now a tree—you can make a tree, sure you can! There! That's a tree! Great! Now make twenty more, just the same. That's it! Quick, quick. Good! What? You're not happy with your tree? Hey, don't be so hard on yourself, it's a great tree. Besides, it's just a beginning. You have to learn to love what you're doing. Okay, now we're going to put in the roof of a cabin. See? It's no more difficult than the tree. Good. That's it. There's your landscape. It's done. Now you have a painting! It's yours. Aren't you pleased with it! Of course you are!"

Langevin organized these creativity workshops in every community in Ontario, he and Obomsawin living out of the back of his camper van. People paid twenty dollars to get in: Langevin gave his pep talk with Obomsawin demonstrating, then the participants tried to make a little painting of their own, with Langevin's unsparing encouragement. He also sold art supplies to those who hadn't come with their own—at three times cost, of course, because of the transportation. From town to town, from Embrun to Cornwall, from Welland to Windsor, and all through the North, people beat down doors to take part in these sessions, to become painters. The two men travelled together like this for three years, and it must be said that the system worked like a charm. Everyone who tried it felt instantly transformed into an artist, and with Langevin walking down the rows of easels praising their work to the skies, who could blame them?

Business flourished. Especially in small towns like Azilda, outside Sudbury, where more than four hundred people a year took part in their creativity workshops. Hundreds of people, and hundreds of thousands of dollars. Of course they ran into fellow painters, professional artists, who scorned the seminars as "not worth shit. You're defrauding the public. You're exploiting the people!"

But Langevin was prepared for such criticism. He was a businessman, and he knew how to sell a product. "There are always those jealous souls who are ready to shit on the success of others," he would say. "The bottom line is, they just won't admit that what Obomsawin and I are accomplishing is nothing less than a masterpiece of popular education. We are awakening the artistic potential of thousands of people, stirring their creative instincts, revealing to them the secret, essential laws of painting. Naturally, the professionals want to keep those secrets to themselves. But I want to see them spread and grow, and flower among the people. Who knows? Among those who participate in my creativity workshops there may lurk a future Renoir, a Manet, a Riopelle. All we are doing is expanding popular sensitivity to the pictorial aesthetic. It is more than revolutionary: it is our moral duty! And what's wrong with making a living by doing our moral duty?"

He neglected to add that they sold their own paintings after each workshop. They were always the same: the roof of a log cabin poking up through a forest; little streams filled with ice in the springtime; animal tracks crossing an ice-covered lake. And they sold like hot cakes. People loved them, and they weren't *that* expensive. There were paintings to suit every taste, every décor, every pocketbook. Langevin also owned a small picture-framing shop in Ottawa, for those who wanted to frame their own paintings. And if you bought one of Langevin's or Obomsawin's paintings for six hundred dollars or more, you got the frame for free. Certainly they encouraged the sale of their own paintings: but only because it provided students with an example to follow as well as a handsome work of art to hang in their living rooms.

Once, when Obomsawin balked at always painting the same scenes over and over, without changing so much as a twig, Langevin explained to him that before becoming a painter he had been an exterminator. "An exterminator of fleas, rats, parasites, all sorts of pests. In order to become an exterminator in the province of Ontario you have to have a licence, right? And to get that licence you have to pass a written and an oral examination. I made a lot of money killing bugs, let me tell you, and I learned a lot about selling, too. And I'll tell you something else: selling extermination contracts, selling paintings, it's exactly the same thing. It's still selling. Sell, sell, sell, that's the name of the game. When I got tired of rats and cockroaches, I took up painting. I'd always liked to draw when I was a kid, you understand. But it's no different from being an exterminator. I made a fortune killing cockroaches, I'm making a fortune selling paintings. It's the same thing.

"But I mean, you want to sell, you don't just sell anything to anybody, eh? Look how many people are out there buying Riopelle and Lemieux. Not a whole lot. Most of them aren't up to that level, they don't appreciate that kind of art, or maybe it's too expensive for them. Whatever. What we're doing here is right: we're educating the masses, giving them a taste for good art, a love of painting. We're giving them a start. We're showing them that they're not as stupid as they thought they were, that's the bottom line in all this. And hey, a painting is a pretty damn good gift to give someone you love, let's face it. Say your daughter just got out of university, she needs something for her new office? Wham! You whip her up a nice northern landscape. Or it's your parents' twenty-fifth wedding anniversary? No problem. You don't give them one of your own paintings this time, they already have one, so you give them a painting done by an artist who is personally known to you, right? What could be better'n that? That's where you and I come in, Obom. The price of things today, four hundred dollars is nothing. It's less than a new washing machine, for Christ's sake. And it's a painting, Obom. It's not something you stick in the basement, like a washing machine. It's right up there on the living room wall. It tells people you've got taste, an artistic sensibility. Everybody does.You just have to develop it, bring it out. And hey, we've got a right to make a living just like everybody else. What's wrong with doing it by educating people, giving them something that'll last? Eh? Like art?

"Speaking of which, I hear Inuit and Indian art is going to get very big in the near future. Ever feel tempted to try it? You've got an Indian name, maybe it could come in handy. You should think about it ...."

Today even Obomsawin will admit that the idea of delving into Amerindian art came to him first from Langevin, the exterminator turned painter.

15

Since Obomsawin's trial began, Sioux Junction has once again become a thriving town.

There are, of course, the judge, the lawyers and the journalists, the people who put Sioux Junction on the map. But there are also scores of tourists, people who never before thought of setting foot in a place like Sioux Junction. Most of these are fans of Obomsawin, some are collectors, others are simply the idly curious. With the return of the whites, who spend money like water, the liquor store reopened practically overnight, and the sudden availability of alcohol has lured the Indians in from the reserve. There is money to make: tourists, after all, like to buy original handcrafted souvenirs to take back home to prove to their friends that they really have been where they said they were going.

There are other types in town as well, but no one knows what they're doing here. The couple from Ottawa, for example, a Mr. and Mrs. Hartfelt, both doctors originally from Germany. As soon as the trial began to appear in the papers, the Hartfelts wrote to Obom's lawyer offering to appear as witnesses for the defence. They arrived a few days ago. Not a bad-looking couple, in their early sixties. Of all the experts who have trooped in front of Judge Kendrick explaining the darker meanings in the works of Thomas Obomsawin, these two have been the most eloquent. Their testimony ate up two whole days. They went through the entire history of Amerindian painting in Canada. According to them, the more Amerindian the painting, the more it approaches the pantheon of true art, and the first works of Obom, the ones he completed when he first took up painting, are among the most significant contributions to Amerindian painting they have ever seen, and certainly the best things he has ever done in his career. They're real experts, too, highly respected and totally objective. Curiously, though, they never mentioned Obom's most lucrative period, when he was teamed up with the cockroach killer turned painter from Ottawa. And they offered no opinion as to the value of Obom's huge historical tableaux, the ones that were burned in the fire and which they had never seen. So they could not say whether or not the fire had destroyed any great contributions to Canadian heritage.

While we're on the subject of expert witnesses, though, no one has seen hide nor hair of Obomsawin's two former biographers.

The Indians who have flocked into Sioux Junction are not all souvenir hawkers and drunks. There are other native painters as well. Among them is Francine Cree, who is becoming better and better known for her watercolours. And Jim Whiteduck, of course, who has had at least a half-dozen biographies written about him already. He paints full time, and his fame is assured. He's a giant of a man—a full-blooded Sioux—who spent time in prison as a young man for raping his sister. It was in prison that he learned how to paint. He lives in Manitoba, deep in the woods and far from the reach of the law. These days he is often seen sitting with Obom on the bench; apart from the Great Depression, he's the only person

Obom ever allows to do so. He acts as a kind of bodyguard. And the
Great Depression is the only person who can walk up to Obom
without being loomed over by the imposing bulk of Jim Whiteduck.
Everyone else, especially the tabloid journalists, have to keep clear
of the bench altogether: Jim is a good sort, usually, but when he's
provoked, or when he has had a few drinks, look out.

There've been the usual complaints about the Indians. People
say they live like savages, that they break things up when they drink,
that they're dirty, that they are illegally occupying those nice
company houses and tearing them to pieces. But most of them have
pitched their tents on the outskirts of town. They sell a few souvenirs to tourists, and keep pretty much to themselves.

Among those who have come to Sioux Junction, but not for the
trial, is a man named Carl Bentham, a businessman from Winnipeg
who was recently mentioned in *Maclean's* magazine. He is, apparently, an entrepreneurial genius who has already made millions in
real estate. His latest masterstroke is acquiring entire towns that
were abandoned after the closing down of mines and then reselling
them house by house at public auction. He pays a thousand dollars
each for the houses and sells them for at least five times that,
transport included, to people who want a summer cottage or an
inexpensive house they can move to wherever the economy is
booming at the time. So far his scheme has worked twice: once in
Saskatchewan and once in northern Quebec, in Schefferville, after
the Iron Ore Company pulled out. Both times he made tons of
money. It's a simple scheme, once you think of it. And it looks as
though Sioux Junction will be up for grabs pretty soon. Bentham
knows his stuff: for him, there's money to be made here, but he has
to be careful. The publicity generated by the trial is good, but first
he has to buy the houses from the Sauvés, who still own the sawmill
as well as the houses built by the mining company. While he waits

for the right moment, Bentham is occupying a hundred-dollar-a-day suite at the Logdrivers Hotel. No one knew that the Logdrivers had such a thing, but apparently that's what he's paying.

The trial has been going pretty well from Obomsawin's point of view, too. At first, things didn't look so good, but then it quickly became apparent that the whole thing rested on the burden of proof. Had anyone actually seen Obomsawin set fire to the house, for example? The only witness who would swear that he had was Roland Provençal. How, then, had Obom gone about it? What did he use to light it? And what exactly was burned? How many paintings had been in the house? And so on.

The chief fire marshal for the province of Ontario came to Sioux Junction personally to testify. In his report to the judge, he declared that the fire had been deliberately set, that much was certain, by throwing gasoline onto several of Obomsawin's paintings, especially a large, historical mural, and then setting a match to them. The paintings had caught first, of that there was no doubt, and the fire had quickly spread to the rest of the house, which had been made almost entirely of logs. The whole building had burned to the ground in less than an hour. The glow from it could be seen for miles, and had attracted the attention of the first Indians returning to Sioux Junction. All that anyone could say about Obomsawin's role in the affair was that he had been found standing in front of the inferno, saying not a word, his face blackened and his jacket slightly scorched. And when Jo Constant had asked him if he had set fire to his mother's house, he had said yes. But he had also been totally drunk at the time, so it was not necessary to believe anything he had said.

"A confession of guilt!" shouted the Crown prosecutor, who at first had wanted a quick trial and an early conviction in his back pocket.

"Objection, Your Honour!" cried the defence attorney. "The defendant was in a state of insobriety. His confession is therefore inadmissable."

"Objection sustained."

It was at this point that Roland Provençal, the prosecution's most important eyewitness, became tangled up in the business. He arrived at the court looking very snappy in his three-piece suit. He had even taken a bath the night before, in order to make a good impression. He was beside himself: his day in the sun had come; he was going to stand up in front of the whole town, he might even get his name in newspapers right across North America. Interviews on the radio, maybe even TV ....

"Yes, Your Honour, I did see Thomas Obomsawin coming out of the house. It was already burning. I'm positive; I was standing right across the road. He seemed very pleased with himself. I know the man very well; you might say it was me who raised him. And I can tell you this: he's an ingrate, a goddamned ingrate."

"Objection, Your Honour. The witness is straying from the question. We're not discussing the accused's moral character at this point. The witness should stick to the facts of the case and spare us his personal reflections."

"Objection sustained."

"Objection or no objection," said Provençal, "Obom is a goddamned ungrateful son of a bitch. I had big plans for that house, I was going to turn it into a museum. I thought it would be good for tourism around here. A lot of people seem to like Obom's pictures. I can't see it, myself, but I thought if they're stupid enough to like the pictures maybe they're stupid enough to come all the way up here to see them. It could've got tourism going in this town, and tourism means jobs for a hell of a lot of people. I know, I ran a hotel for seven years once, and I know what I'm talking about. But oh no ... this goddamned ungrateful son of a bitch has to go and burn down his own mother's house ...."

16

His first time? Obom remembers it as if it were yesterday.

It was with Carmen Richer, who was more beautiful than a summer's day. She and Thomas saw each other as often as possible, which is to say once every two weeks when Thomas came down from the Sauvé brothers' lumber camp in Keegstra, about six hundred kilometres north of Sioux Junction. That summer Thomas was working in the woods, as was almost everyone else. His employers liked him well enough, and even offered him a job at the planing mill starting in the fall, with the promise of a desk job later on. His field boss, a man named Rancourt, told him that if he wanted to he could spend his whole life working in forestry: the industry paid well, promotions came easily, and who knows, he might even be a field boss himself some day. Then he could get married, make a normal life for himself, have children, buy a house. Obom listened to all this without comment, because he liked Rancourt, who had taken him on when no one else would. But the field boss was driven by a single idea: to give Obomsawin a chance in life, to change him, to make something out of him. After all, as everyone knew, Obom had just come out of reform school in Alfred.

"Thomas, my boy, you listen to old Rancourt," he would say. "Old Rancourt knows what's what. He'll make a man out of you yet. He's dealt with harder cases than you."

To which Thomas would nod, or smile shyly, and say, "Yes sir, M. Rancourt, I know."

"And don't forget, Thomas, there's only two things in life worth knowing. How to make a living, and how to raise a family to be good Christians. Don't never forget that."

Raise a family, earn a living. These things left a bitter taste in Tom's mouth, like his first cigarette. That summer there were two quite different thoughts uppermost in Obom's mind: to save enough money to buy art supplies and to sleep with Carmen. He intended to leave Sioux Junction in the fall, move to Toronto or Montreal, set up a studio and paint all day every day.

Thomas had known Carmen forever; they had grown up together, lived in the same neighbourhood. She had always come first in her class; her parents had money, and she was the best looking of all the Richer sisters. She was going back to the convent in the fall, everyone knew that. And she liked Thomas Obomsawin; only she and Thomas knew that, but that was plenty.

Throughout the summer Thomas never breathed a word about Carmen to another soul. She kept quiet about it, too. The only way I know about it now is because he told me himself, much later, as his third biographer.

The couple had good reason to keep their affair to themselves. Thomas wasn't one of Sioux Junction's favourite sons. He had spent four years in a reform school in Alfred, about fifty kilometres from Ottawa, for having set fire to Sioux Junction's primary school. It's not a particularly edifying story, but here it is: Thomas broke into the school one night after everyone had gone home. In those days, he was always up to no good; he wasn't even going to school any more. His mother couldn't afford clothes for him, he said. He broke into the school to get at the bottle of wine the caretaker kept in his locker. He wasn't alone. Two other boys were with him: Wayne Wabaschi, another Sioux from the reserve, and Jean-Charles Sigouin, whose father was a miner. Exactly how they got in was never discovered, but once they found the wine they took a few swigs, smoked a few cigars, played cards for a while. The fire started in one of the wastebaskets. Thomas was the only one to turn himself in; he took the rap for the others, and he never told anyone who they were.

Up to that point, Obom had a clean record. His mother wasn't working at the time; she was drinking heavily and seeing a lot of different men, even though she was living with Larry. The social worker explained to the judge that removing an adolescent from the influence of such a mother probably wasn't a bad idea, and even Flore agreed with her. Since her little boy was returned to her from his sojourn in the United States, she had found that he wasn't really her little boy any more, that he had changed into someone else entirely. She didn't protest at all, not even when the family court judge decided to send Thomas to the reform school in Alfred. Maybe he would learn a trade there, she thought, and be able to earn a living when he got out. And maybe he'd learn how to get along with people, make friends. It'd do him good. Besides, Larry was beginning to get tired of having Obom around all the time. He and Flore planned to move out west, to make a new life for themselves, and there was no question of their taking Obom with them.

So when it came right down to it, as Obomsawin says today, that fire turned out to be a good thing for everyone. His parents got rid of him, the judge cleansed the town of a future juvenile delinquent, and the school board got a whopping big insurance settlement that allowed them to build a nice new school without costing the local taxpayers a cent. And that wasn't all: at the reform school, which was run by the Christian Brothers, Thomas learned how to draw.

"There were two brothers there who taught art," says Obom. "Brother Marius and Brother Isaiah. Looking back on it now, I can see that they were a couple of ignoramuses who were doing their best, that they'd been told to teach drawing even though they knew absolutely nothing about it. But they threw themselves into it anyway. I spent all my time sketching with them. They thought I had a gift, but more than that, they liked me because I behaved myself with them, I didn't cause any trouble. As for me, I loved to draw, and somehow I knew that these guys weren't so bad, that they weren't there to reform me, but to help me.

"So I spent four good years there. We had three meals a day, for one thing, and when you think about it there weren't many of us there who were used to that. The food wasn't exactly five-star, but it was better than nothing. And we got our clothes free and slept in warm beds at night. It never even occurred to me to run away. I could have been released after two years because of good behaviour, but I didn't want to leave. The only thing about the place that was hard to take was the other kids. Most of them had been beaten up at home all their lives, and just wanted to beat up on everyone else in return. But in any case, I got to draw as much as I liked any time I liked, so what the hell ....

"Brother Marius encouraged me most. The first time I ever went to the National Gallery in Ottawa was with him. He wanted to show me some real paintings. And man, I'll remember that trip as long as I live. They had every kind of painting you could think of: nudes, abstracts, paintings from Germany, Italy, the States. It was that day I decided I was going to devote the rest of my life to painting.

"One day Brother Isaiah said to me, 'If you like to paint so much I'll introduce you to a friend of mine who's a painter in Ottawa.' This was Langevin, who I've already told you about. 'He's a guy who makes paintings,' said Brother Isaiah, 'but he makes a lot of money at it. He's a real businessman. He runs at least two companies in his wife's name.' Langevin must be getting on in age, now, and he's rolling in dough and doesn't think about anything but money, money, money. But he was very kind to me in those days. He gave me a taste for living high off the hog. First thing he told me was to come back to see him when I was tired of starving to death.

"Anyway, my mind was made up: I was going to be a painter. When I turned seventeen, though, it didn't matter how much I liked the reform school, I had to leave. I was too old. So I decided to go back to the Junction, where I knew I could find work and make enough money to buy paint and brushes and maybe buy some time to paint my brains out if I wanted to ...."

"So in other words, you really only spent two years at Alfred against your will. The second two years you were there voluntarily. That isn't what your first two biographers wrote, is it?"

"My first two biographers," Obom spat. "Two buckets of shit! I've never even laid eyes on them!"

"Well, let's not stray from the topic. You were going to tell me about Carmen."

"Ah yes, Carmen."

She had fallen completely head over heels for him. She didn't talk about marriage, of course; she knew they were too young for that, and her parents would have hit the roof if they knew she was even seeing someone of Obomsawin's class. But she was in love with him, there was no doubt about that. She had thought about him every day since the junker festival, in her convent room at Sturgeon Falls; she wrote fifteen-page imaginary letters to him that she never would have dared put down on paper. She could hardly wait until summer, when she would see him again. Thomas Obomsawin. She thought he was the most handsome man in the world, and that she was the only one who could see it.

When she returned to Sioux Junction for the summer, she didn't waste any time. She set out to find him. She was sixteen years old and could do anything she had a mind to. She and Tom sort of bumped into each other one night in June: he was working at the Sauvé brothers' plant, trying to make enough money to take a year off and paint. "That's a great idea, Tom, but I didn't know you were a painter." (It's true, she didn't, but when she found out it made her love him twice as much.)

"But what about you, you're Carmen Richer, you're a convent girl. Will I be able to see you again?"

"Yes, Tom, as long as my parents don't find out."

That night they kissed again; Carmen nearly fainted she was so happy. It was the beginning of summer.

At first, Obom and Carmen indulged in no more than a good-night kiss at the end of the evening. But after three or four dates they began to neck and walked everywhere with their arms around each other. They knew where it was leading; it would be the first time for both of them. If my parents send me back to the convent, Carmen said to herself, I'll sleep with him before I go. If they keep me here, I'll wait. We can be married at Christmas, when he turns eighteen.

"It's up to you," Tom told her. "You decide when. Me, I've been ready since the festival."

For a while they got together at the cottage Carmen's father owned on one of the islands in Lake Winnissogan. They would meet there; she would sail over on her father's yacht, he would row across in a borrowed boat. But then Carmen's mother stopped her from going to the cottage by herself; perhaps she suspected something. In any case, they began to meet wherever they could. It wasn't easy. They didn't dare be seen together. The gossip mongers would have eaten them whole.

In the end they found the perfect place. It was in the town dump, believe it or not. No one went there except the bears, and

Tom had found an old pickup body, completely rusted out, but with a camper on the back that was still in fairly good shape. He tore out the old carpeting and bench covers. It smelled a bit mouldy, but there were no bugs in it. And it was big enough for them to lie down. By the end of July they were going there every night; they would pack in some food for a picnic, plenty of cigarettes, and even a few bottles of beer. To help them relax.

They both felt themselves ready for it at the same time. Oh that felt so good ... ooh that felt even better ... mmm much better. And the longer it lasted, the better it felt. They had to be careful, but it was worth it.

The summer ended. Carmen went back to the convent, her face a mask of grief. Before leaving, she picked a fight with him, and he didn't show up for their last meeting. The imbecile! Suddenly the whole thing seemed like nothing more than a summer fling. She no longer knew what to think.

When the Mother Superior of the convent sent Carmen home in November with a note to her parents advising them to find her a doctor, it didn't seem so casual. Obom had gone off on one of his numerous self-imposed exiles. Carmen refused to say anything about who the father was, even to the priest, who tried to force it out of her at confession. Her parents wondered what they had ever done to deserve such a child.

But they arranged everything. The priest knew of a house in Ottawa where young mothers were discreetly cared for until their time came. One of those big rambling houses on Daly Street, all tastefully restored with BMWs parked in the driveways. Carmen ended up there, her baby ended up being adopted, and though everyone in Sioux Junction knew about it, no one ever spoke of it in front of the Richers. There are some things one doesn't talk about. Not even Carmen mentioned it. What was the point, anyway? Her daughter had no doubt been taken in by a good family. She was certainly too young to look after it, and her parents didn't even want to know about it. Neither, apparently, did Obomsawin: he never asked her what had happened, either to her or to the child.

Today Carmen is married to Pierre Carrière, a young man from her own neighbourhood who has become something of a splash as a diplomat. He's the Canadian ambassador to Nicaragua. They have two children, both of them growing like weeds. She has money (inherited from her parents), servants. She and her husband speak French with a Parisian accent. Everything is just fine, thank you very much.

Carmen was eager to talk to me about her time with Obomsawin. She wasn't ashamed of what had happened. It was all so long ago. There was only one part of the story that still caused her pain, one little memory that haunted her, the kind of thing we all drag along with us in our lives.

She had had her child in March. In the Junction it had been given out that she had stayed on at the convent to help the nuns with their religious ceremonies, and that was why she hadn't come home during the school term. But when school was out in June she had had to return. She arrived just in time for the Festival of the Wreck announcing the first day of summer, the day the ice in the lake began to break up. Carmen was there with half the village around her, applauding as the old truck in which she and Obomsawin had started their baby sank slowly through the ice. No one in the crowd understood why her eyes were full of tears.

17

Tonight we're having a party at the Logdrivers.

A small party, not the huge bash Cècile Constant had in mind. This one was organized by some of Obomsawin's friends. This morning the Crown's star witness, Roland Provençal, screwed up, and the defence lawyer took advantage of the confusion to discredit him in the eyes of the jury. So even if Provençal's testimony is stricken from the record, Obom's acquittal is pretty well assured. And that calls for a party.

On the witness stand, Roland got off to a good start. With great confidence, he told how he had seen Obom leaving the burning house, and had heard him say almost nonchalantly that the fire had started on his own paintings. Hearing this, the jury and everyone else in the courtroom were convinced that Obomsawin was guilty of starting the fire.

Which was when Roland, sensing an easy victory, got carried away. Despite repeated objections from the defence and several calls to order from the judge, Roland launched into his own version of

Obomsawin's incendiary past: how as a child he had set fire to Marie-du-Sacré-Coeur School, and had spent four years in reform school as a result. To hear Roland tell it, Obom had gone around starting fires all over town. "I tell you, Your Highness," Roland said at one point, "he's a real son of a bitch for fires. And he's got a heart of stone!"

Fairfield, the defence attorney, jumped to his feet and shouted that the witness was alluding to circumstances that had not been introduced to the trial, with the obvious intent of prejudicing the jury against his client.

"I demand a mistrial, Your Honour!"

The Crown prosecutor, Mr. Lennox, had to go to enormous lengths to undo the damage Provençal had done to his case. And he almost succeeded. But Fairfield knew a good thing when he saw one, and this was a good thing. Suddenly, as if transformed by a magic spell, Fairfield calmed down and very quietly, very innocently, asked Provençal a few more questions. Provençal leapt at the bait.

All Fairfield had to do was get Provençal talking. For starters, he asked him what he had done in his life. Provençal, suspecting nothing, replied that among many other things he had spent a year in Paris, living with a bunch of hobos under a bridge, just to see what it was like. He had served five years in the foreign legion, then he had worked for thirty years in the Yukon. He was a personal friend of the prime minister of Canada, who often came up to the Junction, driving a black limousine, to ask his advice on important matters of state: IBM and Coca-Cola were on the brink of bankruptcy, a second Depression was just around the corner and the recently united Germanies were planning an invasion of the Soviet Union, which was a damn good idea. And, oh yes, he was a direct descendant of Christ.

Here the judge took off his glasses and looked down at Provençal. "You are a descendant of Christ?" he asked him. "You mean *Jesus* Christ?"

"The very same, Your Majesty," said Roland. And he went on to explain that Christ had indeed been crucified by the Romans, but Pontius Pilate had freed him that night and sent him to Gaul, "which was the Roman word for France." In Gaul, Christ had married and had two children: his great-great-grandson, named Clovis, later became the first king of France. Now, Louis XIV, as is well known, was a descendant of Clovis, you could read that for yourself in the history books. And the *filles du roi*, the women sent over to New France to be settlers' wives, were the illegitimate daughters of Louis XIV. The first Provençal in Canada had married one of those *filles du roi*. So that meant, did it not, that he, Roland Provençal, was descended from Jesus Christ?

There was an awkward silence in the courtroom. The judge put his glasses back on. The defence lawyer smiled serenely and, standing up, asked one more question.

"Mr. Provençal," he said, "what would you estimate the population of Canada to be?"

"Well, I'm not sure," said Roland. "Maybe four, five hundred million. Couldn't be much more than that."

"Thank you, Mr. Provençal. No more questions, Your Honour."

The jury was laughing out loud. Roland was told he could step down from the stand. The judge would surely disallow his testimony. And tomorrow a string of witnesses were due up who would finish Provençal off for good: among them was a doctor from Thunder Bay, named Franklin McGuire, who would testify that Roland had been on welfare since the age of twenty, and had never set foot out of Sioux Junction in his life.

So we're having a party. We aren't overdoing it—we don't want to jinx anything. You never know, it might bring bad luck to celebrate too early. And Obom isn't here anyway. He's too sick. Neither is Dear Ziggy. She's too busy. Mme Constant is disappointed. So we're just a few friends getting quietly drunk in little groups, speaking calmly among ourselves. We seem relaxed. Jo Constant is asleep on the couch: all the running around has exhausted him. The judge is a bit tipsy. He must be: he's chatting up Cécile, who is blushing with pleasure. In one corner, the Great Depression is playing some ancient jazz tunes on a saxophone—the sad old sax that used to belong to Omer, the music teacher.

So, it's a small party, but it helps to pass the time.

18

Everyone here in the Junction calls me the Great Depression.

They won't be calling me that for long, though, because I'm leaving. They wouldn't be calling me that if I stayed, either, because my depression is over. I'm better. I'm off my medication. Pretty soon I'll be going back to my job at the Ontario Ministry of Community and Social Services; I've got a letter right here from my supervisor saying so. I'm being transferred out of Sioux Junction; probably to Hamilton or Ottawa, someplace quieter. We'll see.

I owe a lot to Obomsawin. Without him I'd still be in the Black Hole of Calcutta. The more I worked on his third biography, the faster my depression cleared up. Roland Provençal used to tell everyone that I spent my nights lying naked on my bed, doing crossword puzzles, but he was wrong—about that as well as everything else. At night I'd copy out my notes on Obomsawin the painter. It was before that, before Obomsawin, that I did the crosswords.

When Obomsawin came back the last time, I was dying slowly and quietly, just like Sioux Junction itself. It wouldn't have been long before I disappeared altogether. It hasn't been officially announced yet, but Carl Bentham told me last night (after making me promise not to tell anyone) that the town is going to be flooded next spring when they finish the dam for the new Kinashobi Reservoir. Five years from now, if you want to see Sioux Junction you'll need scuba gear or a submarine. No more Sioux Junction. The town will cease to exist except in the history books. Bentham says now's the time to buy up all the houses built by the mining company and owned by the Sauvés. Buy cheap, sell dear.

Yes, I started writing Obom's third biography in order to find a way out of my despair. And there's something else you should know: I also wrote the first two—one in English and one in French. I'm writing this one, which will be the last one, in French, too—my own French, this time. If for no other reason than that, it'll be better than the others.

I should also tell you that I was born here in Sioux Junction, like Obomsawin and all the others I've been going on about. My name, by the way, is Louis Yelle. My father was the principal of the French school.

I've known Obom since I was six. Even then, people were predicting he'd be trouble. How many times did I hear my father say that Obom would turn out rotten because he didn't know how to take advice? Obom refused to become my father's little Frenchified monkey on a string. He was lucky; luckier than I was, anyway. After primary school, I went to a Jesuit high school in Sudbury, and after that I studied sociology in the United States. My doctoral dissertation at the University of Wisconsin in Madison was on the acculturation of the Sioux, if you can believe it. I taught for a while at various places, then returned to Sioux Junction to work off some of the sins perpetrated by whites against the Indians. My divorce had already plunged me into a state of depression by the time I got here.

But it's all behind me now. Getting back with Obomsawin has helped me to rethink all of that. I can admit to myself that it wasn't me who raped all those Indian women and stole all that Ojibway and Cree land; I may be descended from criminals, but their sins died with them. The Indians are getting along all right by themselves these days anyway—they don't need help from some social worker who has come up here to get away from his own little personal problems. They have their own resources; they have their own lawyers and accountants who can get them out of the hole. Obom once told me that those guys from the reserve, the ones who beat the shit out of me, may have done me a favour, taught me not to be so goddamned condescending. He may be right. In a way.

I never told Obom that it was me who wrote those first two biographies. I was too ashamed. I had good reason to be.

I wrote the first one in English. I should point out that I didn't have much choice. I had just returned from the States; I was living in English Canada with a woman who was originally from India. I was thinking and living entirely in English. I couldn't just pick up a pen and start writing in French. I suppose it was also an act of rebellion against my father, who had been the French teacher in Sioux Junction for thirty years. One of a thousand little ways of assassinating him, of getting myself out from under him. A way of disowning a language that had been used primarily to subjugate people under the guise of educating them, as my father had very clearly demonstrated.

But why Obom? To get away from writing scholarly papers, for one thing, and to repay what I felt was my debt to the Indians. And because there were no other subjects around that evoked enough enthusiasm in me to make me want to write about them. I couldn't write about myself, so I projected myself onto him. I placed all my ambitions, all my aesthetic fantasies, in Obom's mouth. In this book too, albeit in a somewhat more lucid manner, I'm proving that even the most objective biographies betray the obsessions of the biographer more than those of the subject. We can't get out of ourselves, we can't even express ourselves, we have to speak in someone else's voice. We become ourselves through others. I chose to become Thomas Obomsawin because he brought out those things in me that I wanted to get out: he had refused to buckle under the tyranny of the French language. He'd even invented an idiolect so he could talk to himself. And to me he was a great painter, practitioner of an art form that had always fascinated me, and which I had failed to master myself after dozens of grotesque attempts.

When my father received his copy of my first book—*The Life and Paintings of Thomas C. Obomsawin*—he almost died of a heart attack on the spot. An English book! He never thought he'd live to see the day, it was like a slap in the face. To have raised a son who would go out and do a thing like that! He wasn't the first father who was ever slapped in the face by a son. It happens in the best families: Jewish fathers who see their sons marry Christians; Newfoundland grandmothers who find out that their granddaughters are going to French immersion schools in Halifax. Prejudices die hard.

It wasn't even the first time my father had been slapped. He was already not speaking to my sister because she had married an Algerian—a man who spoke perfect French, mind you, but whose skin was just a shade too tawny for my father's taste. My other sister lives in Pittsburgh with her husband and their children. My father, the stout defender of the French language in Sioux Junction, has grandchildren who call him "Gramps." He never sees them. And then I go and write a book in English.

My sisters and I are trying to kill him, each in our own way. So far we haven't succeeded. He's alive and well and living in Florida, with all his old cronies. Every month he delivers a lecture at the local Alliance française on the beauty and necessity of language, of *his* language, to a group of half-deaf fogies, and every summer he goes to Quebec. Friends who see him from time to time tell me that he's never looked healthier. He loves fighting for his beloved language. It must be the struggle that keeps him alive so long.

I didn't write the second biography in French to make up for writing the first one in English. It wasn't as a form of apology to M. Yelle, Sioux Junction's most fervent professor of French. I still think he's wrong: I still don't believe that the French language, centralist by nature though it is, was invented in order to dominate others with the beautiful accents and prettified phrases of great writers who are dead and can no longer speak to us. French has no future unless we stop using it as a weapon of cultural domination; it'll die unless we allow it to be enriched by words from other francophone cultures, even with words taken from English. The salvation of the French language will come on the day that we permit it to include every word spoken by French people all over the world. To hell with "Parisian French," that pablum spoon-fed to us so assiduously by Westmounters to remind us of our subservient position, of our past as a conquered nation, and to reinforce our inferiority complex at not being able to speak our own language "properly." I told myself that those days were over, finished. And that conviction allowed me to go on.

I started writing in French again when my daughter was born. I was married to an Acadian, a woman from Bouctouche, and it was through her that I learned to love my own language, and to have renewed faith in my own abilities. Maud's birth gave me the courage to reflect on all that, and to try again. I didn't even have to change subjects: I was still hiding behind Obomsawin's paintings.

Maybe that's why my second book failed too. It wasn't me who was writing; it was someone else, writing in someone else's voice—someone who spoke better French than I did. Obviously the fault was mine: I had absolutely no self-confidence. I asked my wife to help me; she spoke a kind of mid-Atlantic French. She taught French in Toronto, and knew how to use a dictionary and a blue pencil. She patiently corrected all my errors in grammar; with her at the reins, I was soon using phrases I didn't understand at all. I was happy, though. I felt better about myself, I felt—naively—that I was being reborn into the French language. I was slowly becoming a new person. Under the direction of my wife, who had succeeded in completely yanking up her Acadian roots, I developed a proper French accent. I smoked Gauloises and drove a beat-up Peugeot. What an idiot!

My book didn't exactly take off, although my wife did. Without bothering to say where she was going, or why. I took a job at the Ministry of Community and Social Services in Toronto, then moved back to Sioux Junction. To get my bearings, I suppose, but also to confirm my convictions about the social condition of Indians in Canada. I was such an innocent. I wanted to learn how to understand myself, how to find out who I was. And I've done that, in a quiet sort of way.

The first two biographies of Obomsawin were published under pseudonyms, which is not surprising. I thought at the time, when I was making up the curricula vitae for my two fictional biographers, that I was doing it purely for fun. I was wrong. No matter what I thought I was doing then, I am now certain that the real me, the old, mute me that had been muzzled and hobbled by my education and my society, was forcing me to take those steps in order to show that those books were not written by me, but by a kind of editorial collective that took a little bit from each of me, but ended up sounding like no one.

I had thought a lot about that in the depths of my depression when Obomsawin came back into the picture. He had been away for a long time, and he was a broken man. He had decided that he would never paint again, that he would make a new start on his life, and that he would give up lying.

I was about as depressed as I was ever going to get. I went to see him, and showed him the two earlier biographies, without telling him that I'd been the one who'd written them. He'd already seen them, of course. He told me they weren't worth diddly-squat, that they wouldn't even make it to the remainder tables. I told him I agreed with him.

I could write a better biography than these, I said. But he'd have to help me. I was going to write it in the only language he and I understood well: the half-Cajun, half-French of an Ontarian in the process of relearning his own tongue. Obom thought it was a good idea, but he made me promise one thing: that I would leave nothing out. I went to work that same night.

19

Obom's end is near, there's no doubt about it. He told me so himself. It's his heart. They've known about it for some time now.

"My mother always said I was a heartless bastard," he says. "If she could see how the damn thing makes me suffer now she'd change her tune. It's a muscle, after all, like any other. If you abuse it all your life, if you smoke like a chimney and drink like a fish, well, you don't shit bricks when it conks out on you, eh?"

He's in a bad way. He's stopped drinking, for one thing: this is the guy who could drink everyone in Sioux Junction under the table. Cold turkey. And tobacco, too—no more smoking. Some days he writhes around on his bench like a soul in hell, gasping for breath; then he dozes off like a baby. People are beginning to wonder why he bothers. He doesn't go for his daily walks any more; it's all he can do to haul himself to the bench on the banks of the Wicked Sarah. He'll take a dozen steps and you'd think he'd just run a marathon. Sometimes his blood stops and he goes blind: he has to stop and concentrate on every muscle in his body, one after the other, just to keep the sidewalk from jumping up and hitting him in the face.

I figure it's now or never if I want to ask him a few questions.

"Is it true that you've never been in love?"

"Yes."

"You've earned a lot of money in your time, eh?"

"No. There were periods when I raked it in, yeah, but I had partners, it was never all mine. I'd get maybe 25 per cent."

"What did you do with it all?"

"I lived off it, what else. Stayed in the best hotels, ate in the best restaurants. There's still some money left somewhere, I don't know where. Enough to pay for my funeral, I hope. I've never been what you might call a squirrel, but I've never owed anybody a cent, either."

"Tell me, Obom. Are you really Amerindian? Everyone says you are."

"Well I'm not, no. I've got some Sioux in me from my mother. And I was raised like a savage—I still live like one. But you know, it's a funny thing. Now it's the in thing to go around telling everyone you're Indian. You used to have to hide it, if you could. I don't care, let people think what they like. Whatever turns them on ... "

"So you're only part Indian."

"Still on about that, eh? Okay, look. Sometimes I feel like an Indian, you know what I mean? Like, when I get mad at something. It's like, *câlisse*, like I'm on a slow burn. And when I'm with other Indians, it's like I don't have to talk and they understand me. It's funny."

"Why do you think the Indians count you as one of them?"

"Because it's to their advantage to do so, I guess."

"It doesn't bother you that you've had two biographies written about you by people you don't know?"

"No, not at all. It even makes me feel I can die easier. I'll tell you, though, it's a damn good feeling to know that somehow you can't die, because there are books and paintings around that say you were alive at one time. You understand what I'm saying, eh?"

"Do you think anyone can ever understand another human being? I mean, totally?"

"No, it's impossible. That's what I love about life: knowing that there's always one part of you somewhere that no one else in the world can touch. Some parts of you vanish with you. I like that."

"Are you afraid of the verdict, Obom?"

"No. If they find me innocent, obviously I'd like that. My mother always said I was nothing but an innocent. Calling me that again wouldn't bother me at all. Afterwards, I'd just go on as I always have ... "

"Painting?"

"No. I've already told you: never again. *Plus jamais.*"

"And if they find you guilty?"

"They'll put me in jail. Big deal. I won't be there long. First they'll put me in a mental hospital, then they'll let me go. That's how it works nowadays. A small room in Toronto, a welfare cheque every month, enough to pay the rent and buy me some food. Pills instead of locks on the doors. I know what it's like. It doesn't bother me. I'll be out of it soon enough, in any case."

"You're going to die, you mean?"

"Yes sir, I'm going to die. Sooner rather than later."

There are lots of people who want to talk to Obom. They think he's some kind of wise old Indian or something. Every morning as he hobbles down to the church bench he's surrounded by disciples, myself and Jim Whiteduck among them. There are some nondisciples there too—Dear Ziggy's shit-mongers, a few curious tourists, art collectors who want Obom's signature to make their paintings more valuable. Obom holds court for fifteen minutes in the morning and fifteen minutes at night, and the rest of the time Jim Whiteduck, who stands six foot five in his stocking feet, keeps the crowd at bay. And a good thing, too, otherwise Obom would be swamped with stupid questions, like, "What's the meaning of life, Obom?" or "Is painting an art form?" or "Do you believe in life after death?"

Obom keeps his answers as short as possible. He gives one of his crooked little smiles, then goes back to sleep. And the crowd disperses, disappointed.

20

The truth has to come out sooner or later.

Obom didn't set fire to his own house, with his own paintings in it. The whole trial was a waste of time.

It was me, Louis Yelle, the Great Depression, who started the fire. Obom was there, he saw me do it. He even helped me do it. But he never said a word. Not even when they arrested him; he didn't even tell them then. He just went along with them, as if he were the real criminal.

I've begged him a hundred times to let me tell them the truth. He won't hear of it. He says things always turn out the way they're supposed to, that I was right to start the fire. He says it would have been better if I'd managed to burn all his paintings instead of just the ones in the house.

I'd been working on the third biography—the true one—for three months on the night of the fire. One by one, through bits of conversation and remarks casually dropped, Obom had destroyed every single hypothesis I had proposed in the previous two books.

I had been completely wrong, I had made a mess on every page, every line, my whole life's work had been nothing but a bunch of academic verbiage. But it wasn't that that revolted me: I wasn't surprised that Obom objected to almost everything in those books— I had invented half of it to suit myself anyway — but there had been certain other revelations that I had not been prepared for at all.

I began to have my doubts about Obom the day he told me about what he called his industrial period, when he painted all those tourist paintings for money and called it popular education. I was crushed; I had always thought of him as incorruptible, I had worshipped the ground he walked on. But from that day on I found myself taking a lot of what he said with a grain of salt.

The big break came when we were discussing the famous painting of his that hangs in the governor general's residence in Ottawa, the one called *Gulls over Lake Nipissing*. It's a fantastic watercolour, full of life, showing a flock of birds in full cry thrusting their pure white breasts at the waves, which are leaping up as if trying to pluck the gulls out of the sky. A painting of great power and beauty, widely held by specialists to be a masterpiece of Amerindian art.

"Oh that," he said. "I didn't paint that."

"What do you mean you didn't paint it?" I said, astonished. "It has your signature on it, doesn't it?"

"Yeah, I know. But it was Jim Whiteduck who painted it."

"What?!"

"Yeah. And you know the one they gave to the president of the United States, Nixon? That was by Maxine Ivanhoe, a Cree painter who lives in New York now."

"Obom, are you trying to tell me that you've never painted a native painting? I don't believe you. It's not possible."

"Take it easy. Put it this way—about half of my paintings were really painted by a few young Cree or Sioux artists who were just getting started and were more or less unknown. I sort of gave them a start, is all."

I was having a hard time with his reasoning.

"It's not hard to understand. They were unknown, I wasn't. I had too many orders to fill, I didn't always have the time, so every now and then I'd put my signature on one of their paintings. I gave them most of the money I got for them. They made a lot more that way than if they'd tried to sell them themselves. And I made a bit myself. What's the big deal?"

"The big deal is it's fraud, Obom."

"Hey, wake up, my friend. Do you think I'm the first guy who ever did that?"

"But doesn't it bother you at all?"

"Not any more."

There he was, sitting on his bench in the fading afternoon sunlight, smoking a roll-your-own cigarette, looking so smug, looking like an Indian disguised as a white man in his big Stetson hat, his goddamned Mackinaw jacket, his goddamned Levi jeans, his stupid cowboy boots. Suddenly I hated the whole bloody mess.

"You're a fake, Obomsawin, goddamn it, a fake. And not a very good one at that!"

"Right on."

Furious, I jumped up and left. It was three days before I saw him again. I spent them in my room, doing crossword puzzles, lying naked on my bed.

He came to see me first. He even tried to apologize.

"Were you mad at me the other day, my friend? You shouldn't get mad at old Obom. C'mon, let's be friends again. Come see me, eh? No hard feelings?"

I thought about it, and I went to see him.

"Okay, Obom," I said to him. "I think I understand you better, now. You know what? I think, deep down, that I'm as much to blame as you are. I had this image of you, and it was a false one; I suppose I had to believe that a certain Obomsawin actually existed. I needed you, so I invented you, I made you up to suit my own purposes. And that's just as dishonest as what you've done, signing your name to someone else's paintings. In the end, they both seem to amount to the same thing, don't they?"

"Hey, now you're talking, old boy! Pull up a chair, take a load off your mind."

"So I've been thinking about this, Obom. Listen. Do you know what they're planning to do? You know your house? The Ontario government wants to buy it and turn it into a museum. They want to haul it down to Hamilton, can you believe that? To make a museum of Amerindian art. I mean, I'm not surprised they want to use your house, Obom, you were one of the first, after all, you goddamned idiot. Obom, we can't let them do it! I've thought about it, and here's what we're gonna do, we're gonna go over to your house, you and me, and we're gonna set fire to it. Just like that. Poof! No more lies, no more fakes, for either of us. We can live like honest men again, we can move on. Are you with me? We can wipe out your past and mine with one match! Nothing like a good fire for starting fresh, eh?"

Obom didn't say anything. He just stood up, put on his cowboy hat, and stuck his pipe in his mouth. He seemed to agree with me. He didn't appear to be bothered by the idea at all.

"I don't want you to think I'm crazy, Obom," I said. "I'm not the Great Depression any more. I haven't taken my pills for weeks. This is a premeditated act, okay? Are you coming with me? For the first time in our lives we're going to stop lying to ourselves."

He still didn't say anything. He helped me carry in some rags that I'd soaked in gasoline. He didn't want to take anything from the house as a memento—some linen, something to eat, a souvenir. Not a thing.

"It's not the first time I've left this house with nothing," he said. "Hurry up."

I looked around for some paper to use for a wick. He handed me one of my books.

"Use this. That cheap paper oughta burn real well."

I didn't hesitate for a second. Burn! May your rotten lies burn in hell! Never had there been a more ardent autodafé!

I turned and ran from the house, straight back to my room where I had one of Old Man Kirkstead's bottles of bootleg liquor. I sat there drinking, waiting for someone to come and arrest me for setting the fire. Finally, I fell asleep, too drunk to stay awake. The next day, I heard that they'd arrested Obomsawin.

21

Obomsawin is finished.

He's not long for this world. And he knows it. Dear Ziggy had a doctor flown in from Chicago, and he confirmed what the others had already told him: one more heart attack and that's it. Still, he's in a better mood than he's been in for a long time.

Two days ago Dear Ziggy broke down in front of the radio microphones and the TV cameras. We have to stop this trial, she told them. We are trying to have it stopped now. I've talked to Obom's lawyer, and he's talked to Obom, but Obom won't hear of it. He says he wants to see it through, he wants it over and done with so he can move on to think about other things.

Dear Ziggy came to the bench to cry on Obom's shoulder: Do something, Obom, she begged him. Don't go on with this farce. They want to kill you. Obomsawin was very patient with her. He kissed her on her glistening cheeks, and asked Jim Whiteduck to drive her out to her private airplane, along with her flock of reporters who were busily scribbling down weekly installments in the story of this tragic love affair between the famous star and the famous painter.

Thomas knew very well that Dear Ziggy was playing the whole thing up for all it was worth, even though her heart was in the right place. The public drama wasn't hurting her career any, and it was driving up the value of the paintings by Obom that she owned—and she owned dozens of them.

"Does it bother you that people like her are profiting from all this, Obom?" I asked him.

"No. She has to get on with her life. And she's not such a bad person. She gave me a hand when I needed one—now it's my turn."

"Are you sure you don't want me to go and give myself up? Tell me the truth, now."

"The truth? What's that?" And he laughed so hard he was seized by a fit of coughing.

"Aren't you tired of lying, Obom?"

"No, I'm not. I've spent my whole life thinking I was someone I wasn't, and making other people think so, too. One more lie, what's the difference, eh?"

"Are you afraid of dying?"

"Christ, no! I've had a wonderful life, and I'm going to have an even better death. Wait'll you see."

Big Jim Whiteduck signalled that it was time for me to leave. Obom was tired.

It seems everyone in Sioux Junction is in pretty good spirits. A team of surveyors has been in measuring all the houses in town, under the direction of Carl Bentham, the superduper king of real estate. The auctions have started, and the Junction is crammed with people: mostly buyers and representatives of various transport companies. About a third of the mining company's houses are gone already. Everyone's doing a bang-up business: private citizens, who have picked up a house for less than five thousand dollars; real estate agents, who are pocketing fat commissions; the mining company, which is rolling in dough again; the transport companies, which aren't doing too badly either. Even the Logdrivers Hotel has been sold; Cécile is deliriously happy. Jo says he's going to be bored to death, but the two of them are off to Florida in a few days. Finally.

The surveyors are actually making a double killing: in less than a year the dam will go up and the Kinashobi Reservoir will put the whole town under fifty feet of water. The name Sioux Junction will disappear from the maps forever. I asked Roland Provençal what he intended to do.

"I'm going to live in Hawaii," he said. "I can probably get a job looking after an apartment building or something. I know Hawaii very well, you know; I lived there for fifteen years once, running rum for the Mafia."

"Roland," I said. "They run rum from the Caribbean."

"Well, where the hell do you think Hawaii is? In the Indian Ocean? Don't argue with me, goddamn it. You think I could live in a place for twenty-five years and not know where the hell it is?"

"Good-bye, Roland. And good luck."

"Good luck to you, too. If you ever need help writing your book about Obomsawin, look me up. I've written a book or two in my time, you know."

"Thanks, Roland. Good-bye."

I'm leaving, too. Tomorrow. When my book comes out, no one will want to bother Obomsawin, not when they learn the truth. I'm going to find something else to do. I'm sure not going to do any more writing: I promised Obom I wouldn't, anyway. He said when you run out of ideas, when you've squeezed every last drop out of your imagination, you have to have the courage to admit it and go on to something else. Or at least shut up. "You've done your bit," he said; "It's time to stop. That's what I should've done myself years ago."

So I gave him my word. I'm thinking of taking up music, actually. Roland Provençal sold me his violin for fifty bucks. He said it was a Stradivarius. I let on I believed him, just to keep him quiet.

We're expecting a verdict any day now. Everyone's getting impatient, even the judge and the two lawyers, now that the summer holidays are nearly over. Yesterday we heard on the radio that the Crown prosecutor in the trial of Thomas Obomsawin has been made a judge in the criminal court in North Bay. The defence lawyer has landed on his feet as well: a big law firm in Hamilton has offered him a job in their litigation department, with a huge salary. Judge Kendrick told us at the hotel that he's going back to his family. Everyone seems happy. I don't think I'll even stick around for the end of the trial. I've had enough of it, too.

I'm eating my last meal at the Logdrivers. Canada goose soup, pork and beans, caribou meat loaf, kiwi pie and a big water glass full of Canadian wine. August is over; there was frost on the ground this morning. It's settled: I'm leaving tomorrow with Jo, who has some errands to run in Thunder Bay. I'm alone in the dining room, which is unusual for this time of day. Except for Cécile, of course, but she never pays any attention to me. As far as she's concerned, I'm still the Great Depression.

Yesterday, Obom told me one last thing that I felt I had to take down. I told him I'd like to know why he never left his church bench, even when it rained, or when it got colder than hell.

"This is where I can breathe in life, great gulps of it," he said. "You wouldn't understand. D'you remember what I told you, about the first time with Carmen? For the first time in our lives we'd found something outside ourselves to love, each other, two innocents. We were happy as children. Lying on that bed in the old truck, the windows shut because of the mosquitoes, holding onto each other, and all of a sudden she says: Do you notice how a man's sex smells the same as a woman's, especially now, after we've made love? Okay,

okay, everybody knows that. But we learned it for ourselves that night.

"And later, when I finally got away from Canada, four or five years and about the same number of fuck-ups after Carmen, I remember being beside the sea for the first time and—you don't have to believe this if you don't want to, but I damn near fainted I was so happy to be alive. It was her smell, my smell, our smell, the smell of two people in love. When I breathed in that sea air, I understood, stupid and naive though I was, that we are all made of water and come from the sea. That smell is our lingering memory of the dark night of time, when we were still half dinosaurs. Do you know what I'm saying, my friend? Let's just say there're enough unhappy people around who will tell you that love sucks!

"Your Obom is going to die, there's no sense kidding ourselves. When I come here to this bench, I wait for the river to calm down. Sometimes the water seems to fill with fish, and they send up a smell that reminds me so much of the sea, it makes me think about life, my friend! I breathe in that smell to the bottom of my soul. And I feel like the happiest man alive ..."

Cécile leaves the dining room for a moment, then comes running back in.

"It's over!" she yells. "The trial, it's finished. We can all leave!!"

I run outside. The whole town is out in the street. The courtroom has emptied, everyone is rushing down to the Wicked Sarah to tell Obomsawin, sitting on his pew. The idly curious, tourists, the purchasers of dream homes, witnesses, reporters, art dealers, the jury, everyone crying out at once: "Obomsawin, come with us! You're not guilty any more, Obom! You're a free man! Come on, let's celebrate!"

I run with them. Someone in the crowd tells me that Obom has been acquitted, the jury was not convinced beyond a reasonable doubt. Obomsawin is innocent! We have to run to tell him right away, he'll be so happy! Even the judge and the two lawyers are happy. They're at the front of the crowd; they look a bit out of place with their long black robes flapping in the wind.

On the way, the Crown prosecuter tells me he won't be launching an appeal. This business has gone on long enough, he says. It's out of his hands, anyway. Mme Constant says she's going to throw a big party later tonight: there'll be caribou steaks, bootleg wine and kiwi tarts for everyone, on the house. Roland Provençal says he knew it would end this way, he always thought Obom was too nice a guy to set fire to his mother's house.

We arrive at the bench on the banks of the Wicked Sarah, with me shouting like a madman—me, the Great Depression, who hasn't said four words to anyone in town for months: "Obom! Come on! Everything's okay, Obom, the past is erased, we can start again at square one! You can paint again! I can rewrite your whole life now!"

We arrive at the bench, the whole town, with the three black robes getting there first. We want to congratulate him. We want to help him get back on his feet. We want to make him our hero.

We find a small circle of Indians standing around the bench. Jim Whiteduck is holding Obom in his arms.

We think Obom is asleep in Jim Whiteduck's arms. Altogether, we shout: "Wake up, Obomsawin! You've won! It's all over!" There is no response from Obom. Jim Whiteduck is caressing his face. Obom is smiling.

Obom is dead. Obomsawin is famous. Obomsawin is immortal.